Books in The Inn at Magnolia Harbor series

Library of Congress-in-Publication Data
Joyful Beginnings / by Elizabeth Penney
p. cm.
I. Title
2019954567

AnniesFiction.com
(800) 282-6643
The Inn at Magnolia Harbor™
Series Creator: Shari Lohner
Editor: Lorie Jones
Cover Illustrator: Bonnie Leick

10 11 12 13 14 | Printed in China | 9 8 7 6 5 4 3 2 1

1

Grace

Grace Porter opened the curtains wide for a view of Lake Haven, her first ritual of the day at the Magnolia Harbor Inn. Not that she was the first one to rise each morning. That would be her younger sister, Charlotte Wylde, the inn's chef.

The sisters had bought the inn, a magnificent antebellum mansion, many years ago, a move that meant returning to Magnolia Harbor, South Carolina. Grace hadn't regretted the decision a single moment since.

A glittering world of sunlight on frost greeted Grace, and she gasped. Winston, her shih tzu mix, lifted his head in inquiry.

"It's all right, boy," she said with a laugh. "It wasn't the view I expected. That's all." Although the temperatures in January averaged around sixty degrees, the forecasters had warned that freezing temperatures might head their way. Apparently, they had arrived.

What did this mean for their guests? They had a full house coming in today to participate in the New Year, New You women's retreat.

With a sigh, Grace grabbed her phone and checked the weather report. She was glad that the temperature was supposed to rise with the sun and melt the frost. Here in the South, close to coastal Charleston, towns and road crews didn't have the equipment or treatments used in places that got more snow. A couple of inches meant slippery roads that could shut down a town for days.

Grace skipped ahead, reading the rest of the forecast. *Oh my.* Actual snow flurries were slated to fall this afternoon. Well, as long as everyone was here and tucked into their rooms, they would be fine. She could light the gas fires and serve hot cocoa to make the place extra cozy.

Eager to share this news with Charlotte, Grace showered and dressed, then walked to the kitchen, Winston at her heels. Though they didn't have any guests yet, she wasn't surprised to see Charlotte already working.

Her sister glanced up from a cookbook she was perusing. "Coffee's ready. And I've got a batch of cinnamon scones in the oven." Despite the early hour, Charlotte looked fresh and pretty, dressed in a pink shirt that flattered her blonde hair and brown eyes. She wore an apron to protect her clothes.

"The scones smell delicious." Grace took an appreciative sniff as she filled a mug with coffee. "What do you think of the weather this morning?"

"I'm glad that I wore my boots. The grass was slippery in places." Charlotte lived in a cottage on the property.

Grace added milk and stirred, then took the first reviving sip of coffee. "We're getting snow this afternoon. Probably only a dusting."

"Really?" Charlotte frowned. "I hope all the guests make it here first."

"Me too." Grace set her mug down to attend to the next important task—feeding Winston. She filled his bowl with kibble, and after the rattling noise stopped, she said, "They're supposed to arrive midday, so it should be fine."

Winston wagged his tail and began eating.

Charlotte leafed through a recipe box. "I should make beef stew tonight and a few loaves of bread." Normally the inn served only breakfast and hors d'oeuvres during the evening social hour. But for this group, they'd agreed to provide a few dinners.

Grace took a seat at the island. "I was thinking about offering hot cocoa tonight too."

The menu for the rest of the week featured lots of vegetables and light protein. Not that the retreat was a weight-loss program, but it had a focus on clean eating. Charlotte was giving cooking lessons as part of the curriculum. Maya Channing, renowned speaker and life coach, was leading the main program. It had been her suggestions that shaped the menu.

"Cold weather requires comfort food." Charlotte grinned. "And it's such a rare occasion that I want to make the most of it."

Also a cookbook author, Charlotte was finishing up her latest project called *Comfort and Cheer from Magnolia Harbor Inn*. The cookbook would showcase her unique recipes and stunning photographs of meals at the inn. Charlotte had published several cookbooks, and they sold copies at the front desk.

A timer dinged, and Charlotte flew to the oven, where she donned mitts and pulled out a tray of fragrant scones. "They'll be ready in a few minutes."

Grace's mouth was watering. "I can't wait." She took another sip of coffee—a rich, dark blend that was Charlotte's specialty. "Do you need me to do anything regarding food today?"

"No, I'm all set," Charlotte said. "I picked up an order at Hanson's yesterday, and Roy is delivering eggs, collards, and winter squash later."

Charlotte created menus using local foods as much as possible, making a point to patronize Hanson's Farm Fresh Foods and small organic farms, including the one Roy Bevins and his family owned.

Grace brought up the retreat schedule on her phone. "This is going to be so interesting. Life planning, massages, spa treatments, and fashion consultation." She was pretty content with her life as well as her look, but it didn't hurt to take stock. And holding the retreat in January, the time of traditional new beginnings, was perfect. A great start to another wonderful year at the inn.

"I'm glad we get to join in," Charlotte said. "I mean, I love my life, but it should be fun."

There had been enough room in the class that local women could participate. Charlotte, Grace, and several others from town were attending.

"You read my mind about the retreat," Grace said. "I feel the same way."

Charlotte set a plate and a container of butter on the counter near Grace's elbow, followed by a fresh scone. "Enjoy."

"Thanks." Grace set aside her phone and picked up the butter knife. After adding butter, she took a bite, the slightly sweet scone crumbling in her mouth with a burst of flavor. "Wonderful," she said around the mouthful. Although Grace liked to cook, she really appreciated her sister's talents in that department.

After Grace finished the scone and coffee, she slid off her chair. "Time to get to work. First I'm putting together bouquets for the rooms."

When the inn gardens were blooming, Grace liked to make arrangements from her own flowers for the five guest rooms. During the off-season, she bought bunches of flowers at Hanson's.

"That's such a nice touch, especially at this time of year." Charlotte removed two big slow cookers from one of the cabinets.

The sisters worked in companionable silence, strains of classical music filling the air. While Charlotte browned stew beef, Grace trimmed the stems of gerbera daisies, lilies, and paper-white narcissus, then added greens to each vase. Winston napped, content to be near his favorite people.

"Good morning," the familiar voice of their aunt called out as the front door opened and shut. A moment later, Winnie Bennett strolled into the kitchen and set two huge cloth bags onto the floor with a thump. She lived nearby with Gus, her retired train conductor husband.

Startled, Winston gave a yip, then raced to greet yet another beloved human.

"I brought the supplies Maya wanted," Winnie said, bending down to pat Winston. "Now I'm excited about the class."

"Me too," Charlotte said. "It will be good to stop moving for a minute and reevaluate life." She divided the browned beef chunks between the two slow cookers.

"Yes, it's important to do that now and then," Winnie agreed. "Or things get away from you."

"Thanks for getting the supplies," Grace said. "Help yourself to coffee and scones."

Winnie, their late mother's sister, was an invaluable asset to the inn, stepping in without question to lend a hand. She worked the front desk, helped clean and cook, and ran errands. Winnie often helped host events held at the inn, and in addition, she was active in local committees and charitable activities. Grace sometimes wished she had half her aunt's energy.

"No problem. I enjoyed picking them out." Winnie wandered over to the coffee maker and filled a mug. "Do you believe this weather? Fortunately, the roads are fine."

"We're supposed to get actual snow later," Grace said as she made a few tweaks to the flower arrangements. She opened a cupboard door and removed a tray, then set the five vases on it.

"Oh my word," Winnie replied. "I suppose snow is rare enough that we can regard it as a treat, not a threat."

"As long as the guests get here okay," Grace said, picking up the tray. "If you need me, I'll be upstairs."

"See you in a bit." Winnie started gathering vegetables for the stew out of the pantry under Charlotte's direction.

Walking through the inn's public rooms never got old for Grace.

She felt so blessed to be the steward of this fine historic property. She admired the spacious living room with its comfortable furniture and tall windows overlooking the lake, where the retreat guests would meet later. And she strolled through the music room, complete with a baby grand piano, and the elegant lobby, which held marble floors, a wrought iron staircase, and a crystal chandelier. All seemed to be in order.

The antebellum mansion had been built in 1816. Two hundred years of laughter, tears, and love. Although Grace wasn't fanciful or prone to flights of imagination, she often sensed that the inn had a personality of its own. Many guests who stayed here left changed with issues resolved and relationships healed. Grace and Charlotte called it the Magnolia Harbor Inn's magic.

Moving slowly to avoid tipping the bouquets, Grace climbed the staircase. She entered the Dogwood Suite, their largest, most luxurious room, often used by newlyweds and those on a second honeymoon. But this week, Maya was staying here. Grace placed a vase of flowers on the corner desk, then set the tray on another table. She smoothed the ivory bedcovers on the four-poster bed and checked the bathroom to make sure it was fully stocked with soaps and candles.

Maya would have a quiet, restful space to recharge between sessions and at night. Grace remembered from her own career days how exhausting it was to present to groups. It was often energizing and exciting, but she'd find herself drained afterward. Hopefully, Maya would leave the inn as refreshed as her students.

When Grace was satisfied with the Dogwood Suite, she went down the hall to the charming Buttercup Suite, which had yellow walls, a king-size bed, and a view of the lake. Dawn Byers and Jamie Sutton had arranged for their friend April Frederick to have this room with its private bath. They'd told Grace that April needed cheerful surroundings right now.

As Grace placed a bouquet of yellow and white flowers with a pop of purple on the mantel, she prayed the guest's spirits would be lifted during her stay. How generous of her friends to insist April stay in here. While the Bluebell and Rosebud Suites were lovely, they shared a bath and didn't have quite the same view. April was obviously blessed with true friends, and whatever her challenges, that was wonderful.

After delivering flowers and checking the Bluebell and Rosebud Suites, Grace climbed another flight of stairs. The Wisteria Loft Suite was the only room on the third floor, and it felt delightfully secluded and private. Shelby Michaels was staying in this room. The view from the veranda provided an almost aerial view of the lake and gardens. Grace paused to gaze out the window at the frosty landscape.

The sky was now overcast, with a sullen light along the horizon that meant bad weather was approaching.

Grace shivered in anticipation, grateful that she and her guests had a warm and safe shelter from the winter cold. Beef stew around a roaring fire would be so comforting on a snowy eve.

2

April

"Here we are." At the wheel of her prized Honda SUV, Dawn Byers signaled and turned between two stone pillars. The car had been a surprise from Dawn's husband when their daughter, Abigail, graduated from college last summer. "The Magnolia Harbor Inn at last."

From the passenger seat, April Frederick studied the historic inn, probably one of the finest antebellum structures she'd ever seen. The three-story mansion sat like a gracious lady in sprawling grounds, tall oaks arching overhead like guardians. The gardens must be gorgeous in the summer, but even under a forbidding sky and with frost coating the ground, the place was enchanting.

"Oh, I love it," Jamie Sutton said from the back seat. "What a glorious place to hold a retreat." The mother of six, Jamie had very little opportunity to go anywhere alone. As she often said, she hadn't even taken a shower in peace since her first child could talk.

As for April, she didn't have an empty nest or a lively bunch of children. But she was bone-tired, both physically and emotionally. If she had her druthers, she would curl up somewhere and hide for a month or two.

As if sensing her thoughts, Jamie tapped April on the shoulder. "You're going to love this retreat. Don't worry. There will be plenty of downtime."

"Yes, it'll be so relaxing," Dawn said. She continued down the drive and past the parking area. "I'm going to park out front so we can unload our bags. Then I'll put the car in the lot."

April bristled a little, seeing this as another not-so-subtle concession especially for her.

"I'm afraid it might be slippery," Dawn explained. "Better safe than sorry."

"Absolutely," Jamie said. "I certainly don't want another broken wrist."

In the mountains of North Carolina near Asheville, where they lived, snow was a common occurrence. Last winter Jamie had fallen in a parking lot and smashed her wrist. She'd told her friends that the only good thing to come out of it was that the kids did their chores without back talk while she was wearing a cast. After that, she'd toyed with the idea of keeping a fake cast around whenever they needed a refresher.

Dawn braked and put the car into park. "Here we are." She pushed a button, and the trunk door rose.

April unbuckled and climbed out, hoisting the strap of her handbag over her left shoulder.

At the rear of the vehicle, Dawn took out their luggage. Jamie had a duffel bag on wheels and a laptop case. Both Dawn and April had roller suitcases.

April pulled up the handle, wincing when a muscle twanged on her right side. But she gritted her teeth and ignored it. What didn't kill her would only make her stronger, right? Though she hadn't exactly seen the truth of that yet.

Dawn smiled and gave April a one-armed hug. Tall and slender, Dawn had short dark hair and a no-nonsense attitude. "This is going to be great." She extended her suitcase handle. "Ready?"

Her friends were uncanny. The moment April felt self-pity or was flooded with doubts and despair, they said or did something encouraging. How did they do that?

"I'm ready," April replied, trying to inject a note of enthusiasm into her voice. A cold wind snaked around the building and down the collar of her fleece coat. She shivered. "I didn't realize it got so cold in this part of South Carolina."

"It usually doesn't," Jamie said. Although over forty, as they all were, Jamie had retained the bouncy demeanor and good looks of her cheerleader youth. She wrinkled her pert nose. "Record cold for a couple of days, according to the forecast. We might even get snow."

"Seriously?" Dawn groaned. "I've had enough of that already, and it's only January." She bumped her suitcase up the steps to the porch.

"It's supposed to warm up again later in the week," Jamie said as she turned the door handle. "They said to come on in, so I'm going to."

April and Dawn followed their friend inside.

When they entered the lobby, April paused to take it in. Polished floors stretched underfoot, with open doors giving glimpses into beautiful rooms. A crystal chandelier sparkled overhead. "This is spectacular."

A little brown dog bounded into the room, running straight to April. She smiled as she leaned down to pet the furry creature.

A dark-haired woman entered the room. "Welcome to the Magnolia Harbor Inn. I see you've met Winston. And I'm Grace Porter, one of the owners. How was your drive today?"

"It was fine. Thankfully, the roads weren't icy," Dawn said. "We're here for the retreat." She gave their names.

Grace checked the computer. "You're all on the second floor. April, you're in the Buttercup Suite. Dawn, you're in the Bluebell. And, Jamie, you're in the Rosebud."

"The Rosebud Suite?" Jamie gave a huge sigh. "I can feel myself relaxing already. I haven't stayed in a suite since my first child was born."

"How many children do you have?" Grace asked.

"Six," Jamie said with a laugh. "Ages two to fourteen."

Grace smiled. "They must keep you busy."

"They sure do." Jamie hugged herself. "I've been looking forward to this retreat for months."

"So have I," Dawn said.

April had signed up only recently after her friends had twisted her arm. "When does the retreat start?" she asked, hazy on the details. She barely had an idea of what it entailed.

"After lunch," Grace said. "We're setting up a sandwich buffet in the dining room now. When you get settled, come down and eat." She picked up a stack of papers on the counter and handed each of them a sheet. "Here's the retreat agenda."

Grace checked the women in and then accompanied them upstairs, helping with their luggage. The innkeeper showed Dawn and Jamie to their suites and escorted April to hers.

"This is such a cheerful room," Grace said as she flicked a switch, turning on lights overhead and the lamps set around the room. "Especially on a gloomy day like this."

April had to agree. The suite had a warm and inviting feel, beckoning her to lounge on the soft bed or sit with a book near the fireplace. Maybe she would forgive her friends for dragging her to this retreat. Maybe it would even help her figure out her life. It was worth a try. "It's lovely. Does the fireplace work?"

"Absolutely." Grace showed her the switch to the gas fire. "Do you want it on?"

"Please." Despite her layers of clothing, April felt cold. She was always cold.

Grace turned on the fire, then showed her the bathroom. "If you need fresh towels or anything else, please call down to the front. Or come find one of us. We're almost always here."

"Thank you." April stood on shaky legs in the middle of the room, craving privacy and the opportunity to collapse.

Perhaps sensing her guest's discomfort, Grace moved toward the door. "I'll be downstairs if you need me."

After Grace gently closed the door, April kicked off her shoes and stretched out on the bed. It was so soft. She moved her arms and legs, taking stock of her aches and pains. Then she lightly touched the surgery site, a reflexive habit she hadn't been able to break. It was as if she were inventorying her losses.

The flames in the gas fire leaped and danced, sending welcome warmth her way. She forced herself to move her hand and focus on what felt good—the mattress, the temperature of the room, the fact that she wasn't riding in a car anymore.

She needed to concentrate on what remained, not on what was lost or her regrets.

Outside the window, a lone snowflake spiraled down. Last year at this time, April had made a discovery that derailed her life.

Until then, and especially in retrospect, she had been content. She was a second-grade teacher with a class of engaging, adorable, hilarious seven-year-olds. She had friends who accompanied her to cultural events in Asheville. She grew vegetables in the summer and took ski trips in the winter. And she dated occasionally.

April had given up on the idea of marriage and children of her own. But she told herself that it was fine. She lavished attention on her nieces and nephews and her friends' children instead.

Then had come the enemy that threatened to snatch even this modest life. Breast cancer.

April, with the support of her friends and an excellent medical team, had fought the disease on every possible front. As a result, she was out of the woods—almost. Next week she had another three-month checkup. The first one had been okay. But she couldn't escape the fear that the doctor would find something. *All better? No, we were just kidding.* How was she ever going to make the five-year mark living with such dread and anxiety?

If she did remain free of cancer, then what about her future? It wasn't as if she could simply go back to her old life. And she had no idea what the new one would be like.

On the pillow beside her ear, her phone rang. It was Dawn. April answered.

"Ready for lunch?" Dawn asked.

No. April rolled over and sat up, every muscle groaning. "I'll be ready in a minute. Need to put my shoes on." She caught a glimpse of her reflection in a mirror. "And comb my hair."

"Lying down?" Dawn guessed. "There's a break scheduled before dinner. Maybe you can nap then."

"Another cup of coffee and I'll be good," April said. "See you in a few."

After putting her shoes on, she shut off the fireplace. Then she turned and walked closer to the mirror. Her chestnut hair, which she wore with sideswept bangs, was shorter after growing back in. Her neat features and hazel eyes appeared the same, even if her skin was pale.

Taking a deep breath, April opened her door and went out into the hallway, where her friends were already waiting for her.

"Do you love your room?" Jamie sighed. "I'm in absolute heaven."

"Me too," Dawn said. "I turned on the gas fireplace for a few minutes."

The fire. April froze. Then she remembered she had turned it off. Forgetfulness was another thing that plagued her. She wasn't sure if it was a lingering effect of the medication or due to her ordeal.

"Tonight I'm taking a bubble bath," Jamie announced. "And I'm staying in until my fingers and toes are absolute prunes."

Accompanied by Jamie's rhapsodies over her room, they went downstairs to the dining room.

Several ladies were already eating lunch at the long table, and they turned as one to smile at April and her friends.

"Help yourselves to sandwiches and soup," an older woman said.

There was a tempting array of sandwich fixings set out on the buffet table. April put together a turkey sandwich with lettuce and mayo and poured a cup of creamy tomato bisque that appeared homemade. Juggling everything, she ventured over to the table and took a seat between the older woman and a young woman with long dark hair and olive skin.

Jamie and Dawn found seats too.

The women introduced themselves to April and her friends. The older woman was Winnie Bennett, aunt to the innkeepers, and the younger one was artist Angel Diaz. They also met Missy Perkins, chamber of commerce director, and Judith Mason, the owner of Spool & Thread, the local fabric shop.

A woman about April's age waved from the end. "I'm Winnie's daughter Paisley Russell."

In the general conversation, April gathered that Paisley was also an elementary school teacher. She was using personal days to attend some of the retreat.

As for April, she was still on medical leave. Returning to work was another hurdle she faced. She both dreaded and longed for it.

Glancing around at the friendly group, April wondered why they were here. They all had friends and family and interesting careers. Surely their lives were already figured out.

An all too familiar feeling of loneliness draped over April's shoulders like a cloak. Would she ever be carefree and content again?

3

Shelby

Shelby Michaels peered at the houses she drove by, wondering if she'd accidentally passed the Magnolia Harbor Inn. But according to the pictures, the place was huge and quite noticeable.

Heat poured from the red Miata's air vents. There was no getting around it. A car with a soft top was horribly impractical in the wintertime. She sighed. Buying it had been Devon Smith's idea. As a rising NASCAR racer, he had insisted his girlfriend drive a sporty vehicle. "When the guys at the track see you behind the wheel," he'd said, "they're going to die from jealousy."

Shelby braked when she spotted a mansion set among tall oaks. No, it couldn't be the inn. There wasn't a sign. A dog came running out, barking loudly, and she pressed on the gas, shooting ahead.

How foolish she'd been to lap up Devon's praise like cream. Shelby was on the short side and had freckles and flaming locks inherited from her grandmother, so she felt like a far cry from the beauty queens top racers dated. Agony stabbed where her heart was supposed to be.

A memory played before her eyes. She'd arrived at the track early, hoping to surprise Devon with dinner at his favorite barbecue joint. Instead, she'd received the shock of her life when she walked in on him kissing Angelique, a racetrack model. One of those perfect, perky women who sprouted like flowers after a rain every race season.

Tears blurred Shelby's vision, making it hard to see the road. She rubbed at them impatiently. How could she be crying again? Ever since she'd caught Devon with Angelique last week, she'd cried every single day. People at work had started giving her funny looks, and she didn't blame them. Usually she was efficient Miss Michaels, junior accountant for NASCAR. But like the fairy-tale romance that had turned to dust, Shelby was finding her job a wee bit unsatisfying.

A sign appeared in the gloom. Here was the Magnolia Harbor Inn at last. Shelby turned down the drive, eager to park and get inside, where hopefully it was warm. She found an empty spot in the parking lot, noticing the number of cars. She groaned. Was she late? The drive from Charlotte had taken longer than she expected. Oh well, there was nothing she could do about it now.

Shelby opened the trunk to retrieve her suitcase and a tote bag of comfort items, including a couple of books, her favorite snacks, a sleep mask, and nail polish. She pictured herself curled up at night, relaxing. Maybe, just maybe, she'd be able to stop thinking about Devon. The memories and hurt were gnawing at her, hollowing her out from the inside.

She'd really believed he was going to propose. Instead, he stepped out with another woman. Behind her back. As she hurried toward the inn, she remembered leaving out a magazine advertisement showing an engagement ring for him to see. A wave of shame washed over her, stealing her breath. Why would gorgeous Devon Smith, ranked number three in the nation, want her?

Shelby walked inside and glanced around. The spacious lobby was empty, but she heard women's voices from a nearby room.

A tall, dark-haired woman entered the foyer. "Welcome to the Magnolia Harbor Inn. You must be Shelby Michaels," she said with a warm smile. "I'm Grace Porter. Let me check you in, and then you can join the others for lunch."

"Sorry I'm late." Shelby unbuttoned the expensive black wool coat Devon had bought her for Christmas. "Getting here took a little longer than I planned."

"You're here now, and that's what counts," Grace said, smiling again.

After Shelby signed in, Grace escorted her up to the Wisteria Loft Suite on the third floor.

"I love it," Shelby said. She went to the window and gazed out at the serene view of the gardens and the lake. "It's snowing." Dozens of flakes drifted down, spinning and floating like tiny dancers.

Grace joined her. "They said it was supposed to." She pointed at the fireplace. "That works if you want to use it later. Many guests enjoy an evening by the fire."

Shelby clasped her hands together. "I've never slept in a room with a fireplace before. I can't wait to try it." Although clouds pressed down, making the day gloomier than ever, Shelby felt a ray of sunshine in her soul. At least she had a wonderful place to nurse her broken heart.

Grace led the way downstairs and escorted Shelby to the dining room. "Please help yourself to the buffet," she said. Then the innkeeper returned to her seat.

Amid lively chatter and a few curious glances sent her way, Shelby made a roast beef sandwich with horseradish and Swiss cheese on wheat. Then she filled a bowl with lentil soup.

The only available chair was near some women in their forties.

"I'm Jamie," a blonde woman said. "And these other two musketeers are Dawn and April."

Dawn gave Shelby a friendly smile, and April nodded a greeting.

As Shelby got settled, she covertly studied her tablemates. Something was troubling April. Shelby noticed the tired circles under April's eyes and the laughter that rang hollow.

Shelby reminded herself that simply because she had a broken heart didn't make her an expert on other people's secret pain. But she couldn't help it. Shelby had developed a keen empathy for others. She was the one who had welcomed the new kid at school or asked the office misfit to lunch.

Her default setting was to ease other people's burdens. That was why Devon had found her such an easy mark. They met right after he had an accident on the track and lost the race he was winning. That qualifying win would have resulted in a spot on the leaderboard and probably more money for sponsorships. He'd been a self-pitying mess the day she'd delivered flowers to his hospital room at the behest of her boss.

"Hello, beautiful," Devon had said when she walked in. "You're just what the doctor ordered."

Shelby smiled now, remembering. Despite his corny remark, she'd found Devon charming. Yes, he was drop-dead gorgeous with a sweep of dark hair and chiseled features, but he had an affable personality and a disarming lack of arrogance.

"So, Shelby, where do you live?" Dawn asked.

Shelby started, jerking her spoon and sending a drop of soup flying. "Um, a small town outside Charlotte, North Carolina." She dabbed at the red spot on the tablecloth with her napkin, her cheeks warming. "I'm an accountant for NASCAR."

Jamie's eyes went wide. "That must be interesting. My husband is a big racing fan." She named several drivers, including Devon.

The heat in Shelby's cheeks went up about a hundred degrees, and to her horror, she heard herself blurt out, "I know Devon Smith." Why had she said that? She swallowed. "I mean, I used to."

Dawn pulled back, studying Shelby's face, but she didn't comment. "Who wants dessert?" she asked, changing the subject. "Did you see those brownies?"

"Yes, and one of them has my name written on it." Jamie grinned. "Or maybe two."

Shelby loved brownies, especially homemade ones. But an image of the rail-thin racetrack model blazed in her mind like a neon sign. One that said she was too heavy and unattractive. "I love them too, but I'd better not," she said, patting her stomach. "Watching my weight."

The other women scoffed at her remark.

"What are you talking about? You're perfect." Jamie leaned across the table, lowering her voice to a confiding whisper. "I used to think I was overweight when I was your age. Now, six kids and more than a decade later, I'm surprised at how pretty I was."

"I can't believe you have six kids," Shelby said.

"Believe it." Jamie winked. She pushed back her chair. "I'm going up for coffee and dessert."

Despite her resolution, Shelby soon found herself standing at the dessert table, exclaiming over the assortment. Besides brownies, there were mini cream puffs, chocolate chip cookies, and raspberry bars.

A blonde woman in her thirties brought a stack of plates to the table. "Hi," she said to Shelby and the others. "I'm Charlotte Wylde, Grace's sister."

"The chef?" Dawn asked. "Will you sign one of your cookbooks for me? I saw a stack for sale in the lobby."

"I'd love to," Charlotte said. "Catch up with me anytime."

A commotion near the dining room doorway caught Shelby's attention. Grace was greeting an elegant woman with sleek dark hair and almond-shaped eyes.

"Oh good. Maya's here," Charlotte said. "I was getting worried."

Shelby recognized the name. Maya was the retreat leader. "What's going on?" she asked April, who was filling a mug with coffee.

"Maya was delayed getting here. From what I overheard, Grace and

Winnie were worried about what they would do if she didn't show."
April moved aside with her mug. "All yours."

Shelby dispensed coffee into a mug, then glanced with curiosity
at the retreat leader. When a friend had told Shelby about the retreat,
she'd researched Maya Channing. Maya was known nationally as a
speaker who encouraged and uplifted without pulling any punches.
She'd been on talk shows and the radio and had published several
best-selling books. Hopefully she would have some insight for Shelby
on how to get her life together.

After lunch, there was a short break while Maya ate her own meal
and prepared for the afternoon session.

Shelby decided to go upstairs to her room. It was as pretty as she
remembered. She took a few minutes to explore, then hung up her
clothing and set out toiletries on the sink. She couldn't wait to soak
in a hot bath and sit by the fire with a book.

Before returning to the retreat, Shelby put on her coat and ventured
out onto the veranda. The snow was still coming down. She lifted her
face, allowing the flakes to dust her skin. Staring straight up into the
whirling snowfall was dizzying, and she had to grip the railing for a
second. She let go with a laugh and watched how the flakes melted
upon contact with the warmer metal of the rail.

If only her pain and humiliation over Devon would dissolve so
easily. Instead, it sat like a hard lump in her belly, an indigestible burden
she carried everywhere.

April

April felt more relaxed after lunch. Her friends always made her laugh, and Shelby, their new acquaintance, was so sweet. April saw a younger version of herself in Shelby—smart and nice but a little insecure, seemingly without reason.

Everyone gathered in the living room for the first session. An easel with a flip chart had been set up, and supplies for the meeting were on a coffee table.

As April sat down in an armchair, she wondered what was behind Shelby's self-doubt. It was probably a man. April used to wear her heart on her sleeve too. But then life taught her a hard lesson.

The quiet hum of chatter stopped when Maya Channing entered the room.

"Hello, ladies," Maya said, smiling. She moved to an open spot in front of the fireplace.

"Hello, Maya," the women said, mostly in unison. April came in a beat too late.

"She's so great," Dawn whispered to April and Jamie.

Her friends were already fans of the motivational speaker, and Dawn owned a few of her books. But April hadn't even searched for Maya's name online after signing up for the retreat. She hadn't been able to muster the interest. Now, as the session began, she hoped she wouldn't be bored.

Maya made a few remarks about the weather and travel, then complimented and thanked Grace and Charlotte. After the gracious opening, she waved both hands. "All right, everyone up."

With groans and laughter, the women stood.

"I'm a firm believer that movement helps us think and learn," Maya explained. "So let's start with a stretch."

The limber instructor led them through a series of movements that eased tension and got their blood moving. After much flapping of arms, bending at the waist, and lifting of knees, she allowed them to sit again. "Now doesn't that feel better?"

April had to admit that she felt a little livelier. Maybe now she wouldn't fall asleep. That was often a danger in a dull meeting, especially after a big meal. She settled back in the chair, ready to listen and learn.

Jamie, who was fast becoming the class clown, put a hand to her stomach with a groan. "I knew I shouldn't have had that second brownie."

The others burst into laughter, joining in with comments about the delicious lunch and how much they ate.

"It's the innkeepers' fault," Maya said. "The food is too good here."

More laughter.

Once the room quieted, Maya continued. "I'm so glad you're all here with me for this retreat." She pointed to the flip chart. *New Year, New You* was written in large letters. "This is the perfect time of year to take stock and make course corrections." She flipped the first page. "And not only are we going to examine our life paths, but we're going to rejuvenate our physical beings." She pointed to each item on the list. "We're going to tune up our eating habits. Get plenty of fresh air and exercise. Rest. Oh yes, sweet rest. And, as a very special treat, you're all getting a makeover."

Applause broke out, punctuated with cheers and hoots.

"Bring it on," Jamie called. "After six kids, I'm well overdue."

Maya raised her brows. "Six? How blessed you are."

A wave of peace rippled over the room at this honest and lovely statement.

Jamie smiled, but tears sparkled in her eyes. "I really am," she said quietly.

April's heart clenched as she fought to contain the emotion threatening to erupt like a lava flow of disappointment and pain. She'd never had a family. Claimed she didn't want one. But what a lie that had been.

Dawn took April's hand and squeezed it. "You okay?" she whispered.

April nodded, thankful for her friend's ready support, although Dawn had no idea why April had been turned upside down and inside out just now. To the world, including friends and family, she was April Frederick, devoted teacher and aunt. She spoiled all her nieces and nephews, blood or honorary, on holidays and birthdays. It was a tradition.

But it was too late to have her own family. April's biological clock was almost out of time. She grabbed a tissue from a nearby box, pretending she needed to blow her nose. Anything to give herself a moment to compose herself. To pretend she was all right.

"Today we're getting started with a new program I recently developed," Maya announced. "You're the first group to try it out for me."

The crowd greeted the news with enthusiasm.

"This course is called Find Your North Star." Maya lowered her voice, speaking almost in a whisper. "And it's going to be in my new book. Do you want to contribute to a book?"

The women almost had a meltdown of excitement over this proposal.

"Do you believe this?" Dawn asked April, her eyes twinkling. "We're going to be part of a book."

April had to admit that she was curious. What was this North Star thing? Oh, she knew what the star itself was, a guide for mariners and explorers. But how was Maya going to translate the concept into real-life terms? The only navigating April ever did was in traffic or in a busy store, trying to get from point A to point B. The thought wasn't very funny, but April giggled a little. It was better than crying.

"Your North Star goal is your lifelong dream," Maya said. "It's what you feel most passionate about. Once you identify your goal, you can take the appropriate steps to achieve it." She asked for a volunteer to pass out sheets of paper.

Winnie hurried to the front, then went around the room handing them out.

"This is the first activity, folks," Maya said. "A tool to assess where you are right now and help you think about where you want to end up. Identify dreams, especially those that are dormant or unfulfilled. And see what needs to change." She paused. "Don't be alarmed. It's not like I know something you don't."

Everyone laughed.

April's paper was upside down, so she hastily righted it to figure out what people were laughing about. *Write Your Own Obituary* was typed along the top, and below the heading was plenty of blank space for handwritten notes.

Her ears began to hum, the sound growing louder as she stared at the paper. Was this some kind of joke? She shot to her feet, barely aware that she jostled Dawn's leg. All she could see was the doorway, like a portal to escape through. She practically ran from the room, feet thumping, her breath coming fast. Her eyes burned with tears, blurring her vision.

Out in the foyer, April paused, uncertain where to go. She glanced at the stairs, but she was out of breath, not ready to tackle the steps. An open door beckoned, so she slipped inside. A music room, furnished with a baby grand piano. She stumbled to the closest chair and collapsed, propping her elbows on her knees and resting her head in her hands.

Breathe. April forced herself to fill her lungs, making her heart rate slow down. She willed her tight muscles to unclench and her hunched shoulders to loosen. As her initial shock receded, embarrassment and shame nudged in. What would people think of her, rushing out of the room like that?

Except for Dawn and Jamie, the other women didn't know that April had recently faced the very real possibility of death. The mention of an obituary had felt like a slap in the face. During some of those long, lonely nights, she'd thought about what her own obituary would say. How people would remember her when she was gone. If she was proud of her accomplishments thus far. If she was ready to die.

The answer to those questions was no. She'd been marking time, drifting, sort of content but not happy—

Winston bolted into the room and jumped up beside April. Whining, he wiggled and snuggled close to her.

April picked up the dog, since that was what he seemed to want. "You're so sweet," she cooed, feeling a little better.

"April?" Someone rapped softly on the door. "May I come in?"

She saw Maya standing in the doorway. "I suppose." She knew that sounded ungracious, but she couldn't summon politeness at the moment.

Maya edged into the room, an apologetic look on her face. "I noticed you left the room. And when you didn't come back, I thought I would check on you. Are you all right?"

April shifted in her seat. "I'm fine." Her voice was a croak. She cleared her throat, hoping the woman would take the hint and go away.

But Maya moved closer, perching on a chair opposite, her hands clasped in her lap. "Forgive me, but you don't seem fine."

To April's horror, her chest clenched in a spasm, and another bout of tears erupted. "You don't understand."

Winston started whining again.

Maya fetched a box of tissues and set it within April's reach. "Do you want to talk about it?"

April grabbed a tissue and took her time wiping her eyes. "I have cancer," she finally said.

Maya put her hand over her heart. "I'm so sorry."

"I just finished my treatments, and hopefully I'm in remission." April held up crossed fingers. "But that exercise about writing an obituary struck a nerve."

The dog butted his head under her hand.

April was thankful for Winston's presence. Petting the dog helped her calm down.

"Oh my." Looking taken aback, Maya swiped a hand through her short hair. "How could I be so insensitive? I'm very sorry. I really blew it."

"Yeah, you kind of did." Then guilt stabbed. April didn't need to rub it in. "But I'm sure you didn't realize. Who wants to think that a student might be battling a life-threatening illness? I'd rather not think about it." She blew her nose. "But I don't have a choice."

Maya was silent for a moment. "I'm changing the name of the exercise. How does 'My Ideal Life' sound?"

April turned the phrase over in her mind. "Not bad. I can work with it." She gave a shaky laugh. "Now I need to figure out what that is."

"I've been through some challenges too," Maya admitted. "Some pretty major ones. And what helped me was listing everything I was grateful for. Give it a try, okay?" The instructor stood. "I'd better get back to the others. Again, I'm so sorry."

Familiar voices drifted in from the lobby.

"Where did she go?" Dawn asked.

"Maybe upstairs," Jamie answered.

April wasn't ready to face her friends, dear as they were. "Can you please head them off at the pass? Tell them I'm all right and that I'll come in a little later."

"I'll do that," Maya said. She hurried out the door, closing it gently.

April could hear her talking to Dawn and Jamie, and soon the three voices faded.

"I guess it's just you and me," April said, burying her face in Winston's soft fur. "Now tell me, what am I grateful for?"

He licked her right on the nose.

She laughed. "How could I forget? I'm grateful to have a sweet little dog on my lap."

"Be honest," Charlotte said. "How many of you get bored with cooking?"

The kitchen counters had been set with cutting boards, knives, and other tools. The students, dressed in aprons and wearing plastic gloves, were standing at their stations.

"Bored with cooking? I get bored with food," Dawn said. "It seems like I'm always making the same dishes over and over."

"So true," Jamie said. "But my husband and kids are pretty picky."

"Most of the time I'm cooking for one," April said. "I sometimes eat leftovers for a whole week." After her earlier meltdown, she felt surprisingly lighter, almost happy. The fact that Winston seemed to have adopted her was definitely contributing to her improved mood. Right now the dog was curled up on the floor nearby, watching her every move.

The other women chimed in with comments.

"I'm going to teach you how to stay out of a food rut," Charlotte announced. "We're going to try new seasonings and dishes. We're also going to learn different ways to prepare basic foods." She held up a carrot. "Everyone know what this is?"

The women laughed, calling out the vegetable name.

"Now that has to be the most boring vegetable," Jamie said. "What can you do with a carrot?"

Charlotte waved the carrot at her like a baton. "You just played right into my hands. I'm going to show you how beautiful the humble carrot can be."

"This should be good," Dawn whispered to April. "I don't even like carrots."

Charlotte asked for a volunteer.

Shelby raised her hand, and soon Charlotte had her distributing half a dozen carrots to each student.

The chef coached them through cutting carrots in several sizes and reducing those to diced carrots.

The simplicity of this technique felt very satisfying to April. It was almost meditative. In the part of her mind not focused on the task, she enumerated her blessings again, feeling a glow as she listed each one.

April glanced over at Shelby, who stood beside her. Shelby was organizing her cuts by size and shape, from smallest to largest. "That's fantastic," April told her. "You have a knack for organizing, don't you?"

Shelby focused on her work, her cheeks flaring with color. "So I've been told. Actually, I—"

"Your arrangement looks great," Charlotte said, appearing at Shelby's elbow. "Mind if I take a picture?"

Shelby shook her head.

The chef snapped a few photos of Shelby posing with the knife, then took several of the rest of the group.

April wondered what Shelby had been about to say before Charlotte walked over. Maybe there would be a chance to raise the topic later.

After the students mastered dicing, they moved on to the next part of the lesson. Charlotte showed them how to make flowers from carrot coins and create waffle shapes and rosettes.

"This is a lot of fun," Winnie said, lining up several rosettes. She nodded at her daughter. "We can do this with Monica and Sam when they're old enough."

"It will be a while," Paisley said with a laugh. "They're only five and seven."

Jamie had children around that age, and the two mothers started chatting, comparing notes while they worked.

"These techniques can be used for all kinds of vegetables," Charlotte said. "You're going to make your own dinner salad while practicing."

She showed them how to prepare lettuce chiffonade and let them design their own salads. Most of the carrots were gathered in a large pot to be made into soup. The students saved some for their salads, except Dawn. But she made up for it with tomatoes, cucumbers, avocado, and peppers. Fruit, olives, nuts, and seeds were available for garnish.

"I'll never eat a boring salad again," April said as she admired her colorful concoction packed with several of her favorite flavors. Even though she lived alone, she could keep enough variety on hand to jazz things up.

The students cleared the counters, putting the used utensils and cutting boards into a bus pan.

"Want to eat dinner with us?" Dawn asked Shelby.

Shelby's eyes lit up. "Thanks. I'd love to. It can be lonely coming to one of these things alone. Especially if you're an introvert like me."

Soon the four women were seated together in the dining room, digging into their salads along with bowls of beef stew and slices of homemade bread. Cheerful warmth radiated from the fireplace. The local women had gone home, and Maya was either up in her room or out of the inn. Winston was sprawled under the table, and April suspected the dog was hoping that goodies might fall his way.

"Today got off to a great start," Jamie said. Then she put a hand to her mouth, glancing at April. "There I go again. Foot in mouth."

April smiled at her friend. "It's okay. I'm fine. I overreacted. That's all." She noticed that Shelby appeared confused, but the young woman was too polite to ask. "I was recently treated for breast cancer," she explained. "And the wording on the first exercise hit me wrong. But I'm good now."

Shelby widened her eyes, obviously surprised by the news. After a moment, she said, "I was wondering why Maya changed it to 'Your Ideal Life.'"

"I like that better anyway," Dawn said, taking a bite of salad. "And guess what? I figured out my North Star goal already."

The others remained silent as they waited for Dawn to continue, but she didn't say anything else.

"Come on," Jamie finally said. "Spill it. We're dying over here." Then, realizing what she had said, she puffed out her cheeks and crossed her eyes. "You can't take me anywhere."

The women laughed.

"Jamie, stop," April said. "You made me laugh, and laughter is the best medicine, right?"

Dawn set her fork down and wiped her mouth with a napkin. "I can't believe I'm going to admit this out loud." She nodded, as if reassuring herself it was all right to continue. "I'm going to write a book and try to get it published." She slumped back. "There, I actually said it."

The others gave Dawn a round of applause.

"That's fantastic," April said. "I know it's been your dream for ages."

"Yes, I've always wanted to be an author," Dawn said. "Ever since my first trip to the library and seeing all those books. But instead of writing, I became a librarian." She was assistant head librarian at a public library.

"I think that's a marvelous goal," Shelby said. "Do you know which genre yet?"

"Oh yes." Dawn beamed. "I have notebooks full of ideas for children's books. Some of them are based on my ancestors, who came over from Scotland."

"Tell you what," Jamie said. "When you finish your first draft, you can test it out on my kids." She grinned. "I could use a break from bedtime stories."

"Your very own focus group," April remarked, buttering another piece of bread.

"I can do readings at the library too," Dawn said. "If the kids run out of the room, that will tell me something." She glanced at the others. "Okay, enough about me. Who else set their North Star goal?"

Jamie raised her hand, a bashful look on her face. "I set one," she said in a tiny voice.

"Well, go ahead," Dawn said. "I already stuck my neck out."

Shelby giggled. "You're all so funny."

"Don't laugh." Jamie wagged a finger in mock admonishment. "It will be your turn soon."

In response, Shelby giggled again, her pale skin flaming.

"I think I can guess," April said. She knew her friend pretty well, including her talents and her regrets.

"I'll tell you." Jamie folded her hands on the table and took a deep breath. "I want to have a show of my own paintings. Of course, that means actually producing some art. I haven't lifted a brush in about six years." She unfolded her hands and eyed them with skepticism. "I've probably forgotten how to paint by now. So there's my first challenge. See if I still have it."

April had seen Jamie's work, most of it done in college. "Talent like yours doesn't vanish." She turned to Shelby. "You should see her landscapes. Talk about gorgeous. And she does portraits too. My favorite is one of two babies in a bathtub, sitting under an azalea bush."

Jamie smiled. "My two oldest. They kept trying to climb out of the bathtub, so I had to take a photo and work from that."

"Bravo," Dawn said, clapping. "I'll be your first patron when you have your show."

"Thanks," Jamie said. "Now I have to do it. I'll plan for next year at this time."

"All right," Dawn said, her gaze flicking between Shelby and April. "Who's going to bare her soul next?"

"I'll go," Shelby volunteered. "Like I mentioned earlier, I'm an accountant. It was never my dream job, but I make good money and it's satisfying to balance the books." She cocked her head. "Is it wrong of me to want something else?"

"No," the others said in unison.

"Well, since I have your blessing, I'll tell you my dream." As Shelby spoke, she lined up her utensils by height, the bottoms even. "I want to start an organizing business."

"Organizing? As in closets?" Jamie asked. "I could use that. And the kids' rooms? They're complete disasters."

"Yes, closets and toys," Shelby said. "But so much more. Kitchens, pantries, sporting gear, tools. People have a lot of stuff these days, and they need attractive ways to keep it organized."

April thought about her small bungalow, packed to the rafters with belongings. "I hear you. I need to organize and do a deep clean, but I'm always too busy." Or too sick as of late. Some days she'd been lucky to simply microwave a meal.

"Did you always want to do this?" Dawn asked. "I'm curious to hear other people's stories."

Shelby continued to play with her utensils. "Well, until lately I didn't even know it was a profession. Until that television show."

The other women murmured in recognition.

"But I always loved bringing order to a mess," Shelby continued. "My first job, though I didn't get paid much since I was only twelve, was helping my grandfather clean out his office. He was a recently retired professor. You've never seen so much paper in your life."

"I'll bet," April said. She pictured her tiny home office, where books and files were stacked on every surface, including the floor. "I'm drowning in paper, and I teach elementary school."

"It takes a special kind of person to bring order out of chaos," Dawn said. "I, for one, salute you."

"Thanks for your support, everyone," Shelby said. "I feel very encouraged."

April tensed. Now it was her turn. Did she have the courage to verbalize her dream? Could such a dream actually be a North Star goal?

To her relief, Charlotte entered the room carrying a silver platter, which she placed next to the coffee and tea urns. "We have mini strawberry shortcakes for dessert, if you're interested. They're very healthy and low calorie too," she joked.

In unison, the ladies pushed back from the table and hurried over to the dessert.

Charlotte cleared their used dishes from the table and put them on a tray. "Let me know if you need anything. I'll be in the kitchen for a while."

"Thanks," April said. "That was a wonderful meal."

The rest of the women chimed in with compliments and thanks. "I'm so glad you enjoyed it," Charlotte said.

"I noticed in one of your cookbooks that you used to work at a restaurant in Charleston," Dawn said to the chef. "Is that where you started cooking?"

"Yes, I worked at Le Crabe Fou after I graduated from culinary school," Charlotte said. "It was a great experience." She told them a little more about her former job at the upscale restaurant, then added, "I loved it, but I've never regretted starting this business with my sister. It's the best thing I could have done." She smiled at them and left the room with the tray.

After April and her friends helped themselves to refreshments, they returned to the table. For a few minutes, all was quiet as they indulged in sweet strawberries on light-as-air biscuits, topped with fresh whipped cream.

Winston was still under the table. He got up and stretched, then sat at April's feet.

April smiled as she bent down to give the dog attention. When she straightened, she felt Jamie watching her, and before her friend could hint, nag, or cajole, she said, "Okay, it's my turn."

"Take your time," Dawn told her.

April swirled her spoon in her dish, watching how the red juice mixed with the snowy cream. "As you know, well, except Shelby, I've never been married." She glanced at Shelby. "I had a very painful breakup when I was about your age."

Shelby gave her a look of understanding.

She seems to get that a little too well. April pushed the thought aside for later. "Anyway, that's not the point. Except that it made me wary of falling in love again. I always put off the idea, thinking I would have enough time later." Her chest tightened with emotion, and it was difficult to speak. "Well, later is here. And I'm going to do my best—not to get married, since that requires cooperation from another person—but to open myself to love."

Verbalizing this desire was like setting down a heavy burden. Her chest felt wider and looser, making it easier to breathe.

Her friends were silent, and when April dared to look at them, she saw only warm sympathy and affection.

Winston moved closer and leaned against April's legs, providing his own brand of comfort.

"Good for you," Shelby said.

Dawn patted April on the hand. "You deserve the best. So hold out for it."

Jamie was more exuberant. She gave April a hug. "You're so lovable. The men are going to be lining up to go out with you."

April was thankful for her friends' support. She remembered how Jamie had once told her that men sensed when a woman was available. Now April wondered if that was true.

Maybe one heartbreak didn't have to define the rest of her life.

Grace

Charlotte returned to the kitchen, carrying a tray of dishes. "They all seem pretty happy in there." She set the tray down and took a seat at the island, where Grace and Winnie were finishing dinner.

"It's going well so far," Grace said. "Although I admit being worried when Maya was late. I was afraid we might have to fill in until she arrived."

"Me too." Charlotte cut a piece of bread from the loaf. "I'm definitely making this again. There's no kneading required, and the dough is refrigerated."

"That does sound simple. I'd love to see the recipe." Winnie used her slice of bread to scoop up beef gravy. Gus was visiting a friend tonight, so Winnie had taken the opportunity to dine with her nieces.

"I'll make a copy for you," Charlotte said.

Grace turned the conversation back to the retreat. "Anyway, I wouldn't have felt equipped to step in today. Maya did a marvelous job."

"She sure did," Winnie said. She tapped the side of her head. "Got the old gray cells working again, in spite of a few creaks and groans."

"You're one of the sharpest people I know," Charlotte said.

Her aunt accepted that with a nod. "But I don't spend much time pondering life. I'm too busy. However, I decided on my North Star goal."

Grace glanced at Charlotte, whose eyes mirrored Grace's own curiosity. "What is it? If you want to share."

Winnie scoffed. "Of course I'll share." She paused, then said with total seriousness, "I want to be a great wife, mother, and grandmother."

This time when Grace exchanged glances with Charlotte, it triggered a bout of laughter. "But you already are. And a wonderful aunt too."

"Well then, I guess I've reached my North Star goal." Winnie wiped her mouth daintily. "I hope you saved some shortcake for us, Charlotte."

Still giggling, Charlotte cleared the stew bowls. "You bet I did."

Grace started to get up.

"Sit right there," Charlotte said, stopping her sister. "I've got this." She prepared three servings of dessert and set them on the island. "Dig in."

Winston bounded into the room, sliding to a stop in front of Charlotte.

"I think someone else wants a snack," Grace said with a grin.

Winston yipped in agreement.

Charlotte chuckled. "I have something for you too," she told Winston. She grabbed a treat from the cupboard and gave it to him.

"That dog has you wrapped around his little paw," Winnie teased.

"I think he has all of us wrapped around his little paw," Grace said.

The women laughed.

After Charlotte washed her hands, she returned to her seat and took a bite of shortcake. "This is nice. A taste of summer in the middle of winter."

"Speaking of winter, I was glad to see it stopped snowing," Winnie said. "You might have been stuck with me. The rest of the ladies too." The flurries had died down by four o'clock that afternoon, and in the end, they hadn't accumulated more than a dusting.

"We wouldn't have minded," Grace said. "But back to Maya. Does anyone else sense that she's troubled? There's something about her . . . I can't put my finger on it."

Winnie slapped the counter. "Hidden sorrow. I saw it in her eyes the minute I met her."

Grace reflected on Winnie's assertion, deciding it was accurate. "I think you're right. We'll have to be extra nice to her."

Charlotte shook her head in mock disbelief. "As if we're not extra nice to all our guests."

"True." Grace picked up a spoon and nabbed a strawberry. "I feel so lucky. I'm living my North Star dream." She chewed the strawberry, enjoying the burst of tart sweetness. "Running an inn is it."

"Mine too," Charlotte said. "I have a never-ending series of guinea pigs to try new recipes on." Her smile was mischievous.

Winnie raised a hand. "I'll be your guinea pig anytime."

Winston, finished with his treat, yipped again.

For a few minutes, all three were quiet as they savored the delicious shortcake.

"This is going to be a very interesting retreat," Winnie remarked, breaking the silence. "I can feel it."

"Good morning," Grace said to her aunt the next morning. "It seems like I just said good night." After making sure the guests were settled, Grace had stayed up far too late reading a long-anticipated novel from the library. Now she wished she had gotten a couple more hours of sleep.

"I hear you," Winnie said, yawning. "It was one of those nights when I tossed and turned."

Winston trotted over to Winnie and wagged his tail.

"Good morning to you too," Winnie said to the dog as she petted him.

Grace and Winnie went into the dining room. Grace had already set out bowls of fresh fruit, yogurt and toppings, and cereal on the buffet table.

"What do you need me to do?" Winnie asked.

"Charlotte is making scrambled eggs and sausage," Grace said. "Maybe see if they're ready."

"I'll do that." Winnie yawned again as she headed toward the kitchen.

Maya entered the room, her hair still damp from a shower. She wore huge round earrings that matched the purple shawl draped around her shoulders. Her linen slacks, top, and shoes were black. "Ah," she said, rubbing her hands together. "This is wonderful."

"Eggs and sausage will be out soon," Grace said. "Please have some coffee while you wait."

The instructor went to the urn to pour a cup. "I'm glad to see we didn't get more snow."

Grace gazed out the window at a sparkling clear day. "No, thank goodness. It's cold today, but at least it's sunny."

Winnie carried a covered metal pan into the room and set it in the warmer. "Here are the eggs. Charlotte's got the sausage coming."

April paused in the doorway. "Am I too early?"

"Not at all." Grace gestured for her to come in. "Please help yourself while it's hot."

"Coffee first, then breakfast," April said. She went over and poured a cup. "I'm starving. Even though I stuffed myself last night."

Winnie tapped a finger on her lips. "I have something for you."

"Really? Did I leave something lying around?" April laughed. "Sometimes I think I would lose my head if it wasn't attached."

"My grandmother used to say that," Winnie said. "But no, that's not it. Hold on. I'll be right back." She bustled full speed into the foyer.

A moment later, Winnie returned and handed April two small packets. They were single-use toe warmers.

Grace smiled to herself. Winnie often gave the guests gifts, and many of them seemed odd at the time. April's gift was no exception.

"What are these for?" April asked.

Winnie put up her hands. "I have no idea. But you're going to need them."

April nodded, seeming to accept Winnie's explanation, and tucked the packets into her handbag. She added cream to her coffee, then joined Maya at the table. The two women began to chat.

Charlotte brought in the sausage, which had a mouthwatering aroma. "This will motivate everyone else to come downstairs," she said, sliding the pan into its holder.

Grace went to the fireplace and lit the gas. Although they had a good heating system, a fire would provide a little extra comfort on a frosty day like this.

Next to appear was Shelby, looking a trifle disheveled, followed by Jamie and Dawn. The guests from town also filtered in for breakfast, which kept the innkeepers running.

Finally, they sat down to eat, fueling up for the busy day ahead.

The first session opened with stretching and deep breathing led by Maya. "You're preparing your body and mind to learn," she explained. "Release all your cares, and leave them outside the doors of this building. This is your sanctuary."

Grace appreciated the concept, but in her case, all her cares were *within* the building or on the grounds around it. But she put aside ruminations about upcoming meals, repairs that were looming, and the never-ending list of chores. Instead, she focused on this room and the dear group of women.

By Charlotte's peaceful expression, Grace guessed that her sister was also shedding her role for the moment.

"It's good to see all of you today," Maya said. "I'm relieved you came back."

Everyone laughed.

"In all seriousness, does anyone want to share something from yesterday's session?" Maya asked.

People around the room spoke up, mentioning an insight, a decision, or a newly formed North Star goal.

Grace listened with fascination, enjoying this view into the hearts of her guests and friends.

"This is amazing." Maya smiled. "You all have discovered your North Star goals. Give yourselves a round of applause."

The ladies clapped.

"Today we're going to identify our successes and proudest moments," Maya announced. "Most of us don't spend much time thinking about those, do we? We're either too busy or too humble to fully savor our greatness. It's true that we're taught not to brag, not to be proud." She held up a finger. "Lest we fall, right? But rather than obsess over our failures, let's give the good stuff equal time."

"She's terrific," Charlotte whispered to Grace. "I'm so glad we did this."

Grace nodded. She glanced around at the rapt faces of her friends and guests. The Magnolia Harbor Inn on a cold winter day was the ideal place to reflect and start anew.

6

Shelby

Shelby had felt great when she opened her eyes that morning. For exactly five seconds. Then she remembered Devon. Despite her better judgment, she reached for her phone to look him up.

This wasn't exactly the early morning ritual instilled by her parents. They'd taught Shelby to spend time in reflection and prayer and to dedicate her thoughts to the day and tasks ahead.

Shelby hadn't even told her mother about the breakup, since she wasn't in the mood to hear the response. Her parents didn't approve of Devon, even though he'd given them lavish Christmas gifts and treated them to New Year's dinner at Charlotte's most expensive, exclusive restaurant.

"He's nice enough," Mom had said when Shelby first brought him to the house. "But is he really your type?"

Shelby had decided that meant she wasn't good enough for Devon, according to her mother. And that really stung.

So the disobedient daughter was salting the wound by looking him up instead of saying her prayers.

Dozens of pictures had flooded the small screen. Devon and his new girlfriend, walking arm in arm down the street. Gazing into each other's eyes at a restaurant. Attending a country music concert put on by Devon's favorite band. Shelby had been completely erased, replaced by a thinner, blonder, more beautiful woman.

Shelby's stomach had turned over. It was obvious that Devon wasn't giving her a thought, so why was she torturing herself this way?

Now, as Shelby listened to Maya speak, her mind was still half on Devon. It was like having a low-grade fever or a stomachache—annoying enough to intrude. She told herself to cut it out. She must have made a funny face or a noise, because April gave her an encouraging smile.

Flooded with shame, Shelby slouched in her chair. What was that saying? Something about feeling bad for not having shoes, then meeting someone without feet? Here she was, depressed over a boyfriend while April was fighting a life-threatening illness.

"I need a volunteer," Maya said.

Shelby raised her hand and went up to the front of the room.

Maya gave her a stack of papers. "Please pass these out. Thank you."

Shelby made the rounds, smiling at each participant.

"We'll have an hour for this portion of the class," Maya said. "First, ten minutes working alone, then half an hour in small groups. At the end, we'll each share one of our greatest successes."

Shelby ended the round with April and her friends, keeping a page for herself. She read the instructions. *Name five of your greatest successes to date. They do not have to relate to your North Star goal. Then rank them in order.*

Five successes? Hmm. Shelby thought back over her life, short as it was. She recalled coming home from school with gold stars on her papers. That was her first taste of success. Oh, and when her mom would say she had done a good job with her chores.

Shelby laughed to herself, remembering how surprised Mom had been when Shelby volunteered to clean out the refrigerator at age seven. Even at that young age, Shelby had liked the feeling she got when things were in order. She used to open the fridge simply to stare at the neat, clean shelves.

"Five minutes," Maya said, pacing back and forth.

Shelby reigned in her unruly thoughts. How about college? She'd earned straight As and graduated summa cum laude. That was one success. What else? With the sense that time was definitely running out, she hastily reviewed her working life and jotted down a couple of notes. She considered adding her first job to the list but decided against it. Maya had said five successes, but would it really matter if she listed fewer?

"All right, it's time to break into small groups," Maya announced. "Now share your successes with one another."

Shelby was glad when April, Jamie, and Dawn asked her to join their group.

"I'll start," Jamie volunteered. "I was going to list my kids, but that would make six. And I couldn't leave one out."

"No fair," Dawn said. "I have only one child."

"And I don't have any," April chimed in. "So kids don't count."

"Didn't think so." Jamie cleared her throat. "Even though we didn't have to, I focused on my North Star goal." She turned the paper so they could see it. "I won my first art prize when I was four."

The others gushed over her accomplishment.

Shelby eyed Jamie with new respect. She must be seriously talented.

The artist went on, sharing four other successes, including winning a scholarship in college for her work. "Hands down, that was my proudest moment. In addition to the birth of my children, of course."

Dawn put up a hand. "I'll go next. I don't have anything as dramatic and public as Jamie to report. But besides Abigail's birth, I can tell you what has brought me a lot of joy."

"Tell us," Jamie said. "I'm on the edge of my seat here."

"Sorry," Dawn said in a tone that said the opposite. She grinned at her friend. "I'm going to take a tiny step back. That whole North Star discussion really got me thinking." She clasped her hands in her lap. "Not counting being with my family, I'm the most energized and happy when I'm telling stories."

"At the library, you mean?" April asked.

Dawn nodded. "Exactly. When I see those sweet little faces gazing up at me, listening so intently, I know I'm doing what I was born to do." She shrugged. "That probably sounds corny."

"Of course not," April protested. "I've seen you reading to the kids, and you're great."

Shelby felt a pang of envy. She'd never experienced the feeling that she was born to do something. The only time she came close was with the satisfaction of a job well done. Everything orderly. Neat. Perfectly arranged.

"When Abigail was little, I loved telling her stories too," Dawn said. "We'd read books, but I would also share family history or things that happened to me as a child. She seemed to like those stories better."

"You're a natural-born storyteller," Jamie said. "So your North Star goal of writing books makes complete sense."

"Not only writing them but getting them published," Dawn added. Then she rose. "After sharing all that, I need another cup of coffee. Anyone else?"

Once they refreshed their mugs and grabbed some cookies, the women settled in to hear the other two share their successes.

Shelby was still gathering her thoughts, with her measly one success, so she gestured toward April. "Why don't you go first?"

April studied her notes for a moment. "I thought about writing down a teaching award I received or doing well in my master's program. But what it all boiled down to was that I succeed when my students succeed."

Jamie clapped. "That's lovely. I wish every teacher felt that way."

Paisley, who was seated nearby, leaned over. "Sorry, but I couldn't help overhearing." She gave April a thumbs-up. "Way to go, fellow schoolteacher."

"Thank you," April said. "It's especially rewarding when I get students who have fallen behind. I make it my mission to figure out how to help them catch up."

"It's so important," Jamie said. "Some kids get behind and stay that way as they're passed along grade to grade. It almost happened to Brandon." She turned to Shelby. "Brandon is my oldest, fourteen last month, and for a while he struggled with reading. He'd much rather build something than sit down with a book."

"I'm glad he had good teachers," Dawn said. "Like April."

April's smile was modest. "Brandon's a good kid, and he's very smart."

Now it was Shelby's turn. Suddenly shy when everyone faced her, she stared down at her paper. "I put down graduating summa cum laude. But after listening to all of you, I don't think that's much."

"Sure it is," Dawn said.

"You got an accounting degree, I'm guessing," Jamie said. "I couldn't get past debit and credit."

"It's a system," Shelby said. "It doesn't necessarily make sense. You have to memorize it."

Hoots and laughs greeted her comments.

Shelby felt herself blush. "My accounting instructor would kill me for saying that."

"I'm glad you did," Jamie said, her eyes sparkling. "You confirmed my lifelong suspicion."

"All right, Shelby," April said once the merriment died down. "Let's dig a little deeper. What does getting those good grades represent to you?"

Maya, who was doing the rounds, strolling with hands behind her back, smiled at April.

Shelby tried to ignore the leader's presence, since that made her feel even more self-conscious. "Um," she said, stalling. "Good grades in accounting help you get a job. But that wasn't all." She considered her answer for a moment. "It felt like everything was organized in my brain, like I'd taken all that raw information and made sense of it. Filed it away properly."

"You conquered it," Jamie said.

Shelby nodded.

Maya clapped to get everyone's attention. "All right, time's up. We have a few minutes before lunch, so here's what we're going to do. Choose your very favorite success, and a representative from your group will share them with the entire group."

"Mine's easy because I listed only one success," Shelby said. "Do you want me to be the representative?"

"Please," her companions chorused.

Shelby waited as the others decided on which success to share. She realized that she was actually having fun. She hadn't thought about Devon for a couple of hours. That was progress, wasn't it?

7

Grace

The session ended with a round of gentle applause.

"What a wonderful morning," Maya said. She glanced at Grace. "Are we set for lunch?"

"Yes, lunch is ready in the dining room," Grace said as she stood. "And we're doing something different today. A hot pot party."

"What's that?" Jamie asked.

Grace smiled. "Another one of Charlotte's many successes. We're creating individual servings of healthy soup."

The ladies got up, stretching and chatting, slowly making their way to the dining room.

Charlotte had placed individual hot pots at each seat, and in the middle of the table were platters of thinly sliced meat, vegetables, dumplings, and noodles. Other small bowls held toppings such as seeds, bean sprouts, and scallions.

Charlotte stood at the head of the table, waiting for everyone to sit down. "There is steaming hot broth in your hot pot. So be careful. You can choose whatever add-ins you want and cook them right into the broth."

As her sister described the variety of meats and vegetables, including several types of mushrooms and greens, Grace's phone buzzed.

Spencer Lewis, her neighbor and friend, had sent a text. *Hate to bother you. But something's wrong with my furnace, and I have the flu.*

The retired FBI intelligence analyst had gotten Grace out of more than one jam at the inn, so the answer was a no-brainer. *I'll be right over,* Grace wrote. She glanced at the table. *What do you want in your hot pot?*

The wind whipping off the lake made Grace shiver as she walked to her car. Although the snow was long gone, the temperature was still well below normal. She opened the passenger door of her white Honda CR-V and stowed the tote holding Spencer's meal. Along with a big thermos of soup, the tote contained homemade bread and elderberry tea. Winnie had recommended the tea, and Grace was glad that she always kept it on hand at the inn.

She drove down Lake Haven Road to Blossom Hill Farm, where Spencer lived and grew pecans. The harvest season was over, and usually Spencer would be outside pruning and cleaning up the orchard. The fact that she hadn't seen him working outside or jogging the last couple of days meant he really was under the weather. She was annoyed that she hadn't noticed. But she'd been busy with the retreat.

Grace parked in front of the white two-story farmhouse and grabbed the tote. At the front door, she knocked, then walked inside, as Spencer had instructed.

Bailey, Spencer's chocolate Lab, came running, nails scrabbling on the hardwood floors. She barked in greeting and twined around Grace's legs.

Grace was well acquainted with the friendly dog. She greeted Bailey with a pat on the head. "Spencer?" she called. "It's Grace."

"I'm in the living room," he croaked.

Grace frowned. He certainly didn't sound good. She started to take off her coat in the foyer but realized it was freezing in the house. She kept her coat on but removed her shoe boots and carried the tote into the main room, a combination living room, kitchen, and dining area.

Wrapped in a quilt, Spencer was lying on a sofa pulled close to a flickering wood fire in the glass-fronted stove. But the heat was barely penetrating the spacious room.

Grace didn't know what to do first, feed him or fix the fire. She decided on warmth. "There is definitely something wrong with your heating system."

"I know," Spencer said. "I was going to call the repairman, but I thought maybe I could try to get it going. Sometimes it needs to be reset."

Grace was familiar with that scenario, having dealt with tricky furnaces in the past. She opened the woodstove door. "I'll go check on it in a minute." With Bailey watching, she prodded the fire with a poker, then added more kindling to increase the flame.

After it caught, she put in several small logs and one big one. Almost immediately, the stove began to cast off more heat. She closed the door with satisfaction.

Bailey collapsed next to the stove with a satisfied sigh.

"That should help." Grace set the poker on the stand. "I brought over homemade chicken broth and well-wishes from Charlotte and Winnie."

Spencer tried to speak but burst into a fit of coughing. "Sorry," he said when it died down. He drank half a glass of water, which had been standing next to an empty pitcher. "That is so nice."

"What are friends for?" Grace took the pitcher and filled it from the refrigerator. She added a few ice cubes to keep it cold, although the frigid house might do that. "Where is the furnace?"

"In the basement." Spencer gave her a wan smile as she set the pitcher down on the end table. "You're a sight for sore eyes, Grace." He gave her a rueful smile. "And I'm guessing I'm just a sight."

Grace laughed, not wanting to answer that. He did look awful, with pasty skin and red-rimmed eyelids and nose. "You're sick. That much is obvious." She turned the pitcher so he could easily grab the handle.

After putting her shoes on, she flicked on the lights and descended the stairs, which had been newly rebuilt. Spencer had done an excellent job fixing up the place.

Many new buildings didn't have basements in South Carolina, but some older ones did. And this cellar was obviously old, like the farmhouse. Someone had poured cement for the floor and walls, covering dirt and stone, but the area still had a musty, earthy odor.

The furnace hulked at one end of the cellar, a gray box with insulated pipes leading off it. Grace hit the red reset button and waited. Nothing. She was tempted to try again, but she knew that wasn't a good idea.

It was time for the furnace to be serviced. She found the tag the technician left from the last cleaning and noted the company. But she'd better ask Spencer before calling. He might have switched firms.

Back in the living room, Spencer was sleeping, a gentle snore rumbling.

Grace studied him for a minute and decided to contact the company tagged on the furnace. She stepped back outside to make the call, not wanting to disturb the sleeping man. Fortunately, they agreed to send someone immediately.

While she was outside, she decided to check in with Charlotte. After filling her in, she asked, "Do you need me right away?"

"We have free time this afternoon," Charlotte reminded her. "There's nothing going on until we gather at five."

"Good. I'm going to stay until the furnace is fixed." Grace's conscience wouldn't allow her to leave Spencer to fend for himself. "He's pretty sick."

She popped back into the house, shivering, and warmed up in front of the fire. She added a couple of logs, then walked to the kitchen to take care of the food. She boiled water for tea and poured some soup into a pan.

Bailey trotted into the kitchen, looking forlorn, so Grace scooped a little more kibble into her dish and freshened her water.

Spencer slept until someone rapped on the front door. He woke with a start.

"It's okay," Grace assured him. "The repairman is here."

"Thank you," Spencer rasped as he sat up and rubbed his eyes.

"Stay put," Grace ordered. "I'll get it."

She answered the door. "Thanks for coming so quickly," she told the tradesman. "I tried to reset the furnace, but it didn't work."

He nodded. "I'll go take a look. I've been here before so I know where to go." Carrying a toolbox, he headed for the basement door.

"Ready for some tea and soup?" Grace asked Spencer.

"I'll try to eat."

Grace fixed a tray in the kitchen and brought it over. She'd included a mug of tea for herself. She took that off the tray and set the tray on Spencer's lap. While he ate, she settled in an armchair with her tea.

"This is tasty." Spencer eagerly spooned up the broth. "I feel better already."

"Charlotte's soup has magical properties," Grace said with a smile. "Good for whatever ails you."

Grace kept an eye on the fire while Spencer ate and the repairman went back and forth to his van, fixing the furnace. Thankfully, the repair was simple, and soon welcome heat was pouring through the vents again.

"Got it going, as you can tell," the repairman said, checking in with Spencer. He gave him the specifics and left a bill.

After the door closed behind him, Spencer turned to Grace. "You're not going to run right off, are you?" His forlorn expression reminded her of Bailey's.

"I can stay a little longer," Grace said, getting to her feet. "Want more soup?"

He glanced into his empty bowl. "I would love more."

Grace took the tray to the kitchen for the refill, where she also made herself another cup of tea. This time, along with the soup, she brought out a sleeve of crackers she found in the cupboard and a bottle of ginger ale.

While Spencer tucked into the second bowl, Grace told him about the retreat. "Charlotte and I are taking part. It's like getting a tune-up for your life."

Head bent over the bowl as he scooped up mouthfuls, he nodded. "Everyone can use that once in a while. Take stock. The North Star goal is interesting. I must say that mine has changed over the years."

"Mine too," Grace said. "Now it's making the inn a place of respite. We've always known that, but verbalizing it makes it even more concrete."

Spencer set the bowl aside with a contented sigh. He opened the sleeve of crackers and took a couple. "I should have put these in the soup."

"There's plenty more," Grace said. "And when you're ready to eat something substantial, I can come back and make you some scrambled eggs."

"Grace, you're an angel. I hate to put you out, but I just might take you up on that offer." He leaned back against the cushions, the firelight playing on his handsome features.

Grace thought he looked a little better than when she'd arrived. He didn't appear quite so gray and drawn. "No problem. I have Charlotte and Winnie. You have Bailey, and she's not that great at cooking."

Bailey, hearing her name, gave a gentle woof.

Spencer adjusted a cushion behind his back. "Back to the North Star thing. I definitely think you've achieved your goal with the inn. It's a really special place."

Grace was warmed by his praise. "I'm so glad you think so. What about you? What's your North Star goal now?"

Spencer chuckled, shaking his head. "It's so different than it used to be. In the FBI, we were completely focused on our jobs. We had to be. People's lives depended on it, even in my department." As an analyst, he hadn't worked in the field. "Now my goal is to grow pecans and be a blessing to this community. That's it."

"Well, I think you're succeeding on both counts," Grace said. Her face heated and the words hovered on her tongue, but she finally said, "Knowing you has been a blessing to me."

Charlotte

Charlotte loaded the last dishes on the cart. The women had decimated the hot pot add-ins, which was good news because there was very little food to put away.

Dawn walked over. "The hot pot was fabulous. Do you need any help?"

"I'm glad to hear that," Charlotte said. "I'm fine, but thanks for asking." Odd as it might seem, she often enjoyed the meditative, orderly process of cleaning up.

"Well, if you do, we're happy to help." Dawn smiled. "My friends and I aren't used to being waited on."

Charlotte returned her smile. "Thank you for the kind offer."

"We're going downtown during break," Dawn said. "We'll definitely stop by Spool & Thread. I'm anxious to see Judith's store. Can you recommend some other shops?"

"Of course." Charlotte walked Dawn out to the lobby and gave her a brochure detailing Magnolia Harbor's downtown. She pointed out several places, including Miss Millie's, a wonderful dress shop, and the Dragonfly Coffee Shop, where Angel worked.

"Thanks," Dawn said. "I can't wait to check them out."

"Have fun," Charlotte said. "We're getting back together at five."

Winnie insisted on helping Charlotte put away the rest of the food and load the dishwasher.

When they were done, her aunt declared, "I'm going home to read a good book and take a nap by the fire. I'll see you later."

As Charlotte removed her apron, she peeked out the kitchen window to check the weather. It wasn't much better than earlier. There was a mix of clouds and sun, and it was still windy. But she needed to get out too. Her heart began to beat a little faster. She would go see Dean Bradley. He should be free. It was in between lunch and dinner, so it was a quiet time for him at The Tidewater.

A few minutes later, Charlotte hopped into her Camry sedan and drove to Dean's small inn and restaurant on the other side of Lake Haven. The retreat guests were having dinner here later.

Charlotte breezed through the front door and smiled at the young woman behind the reception desk.

Returning the smile, the woman said, "He's in his office."

"Thanks." Charlotte walked to the office and saw the door was partially open. She tapped on the doorjamb. "Knock, knock."

"Come in," Dean called.

When she entered, she found him sitting behind his desk. It was littered with invoices and paperwork.

Dean stood at the sight of her, and his whole face lit up, transformed by a disarming smile.

Charlotte's heart skipped a beat, a habit it had picked up since their first kiss at Christmas. Dean was tall with dark hair and a perpetual five-o'clock shadow. She had always thought he was good-looking, but now he was someone special.

Dean held out his arms, and Charlotte stepped into them, sheltered by his warmth. He kissed her lightly. Attractive laugh lines crinkled around his eyes. "It's great to see you."

"You too." Charlotte nestled closer for a moment, then moved back. "You seem busy. Is this a bad time?"

"Of course not." He glanced at his desk and grimaced. "One thing you can say about paperwork is that it won't go anywhere."

"Want to take a walk?" Charlotte asked. Although the wind was blustery, she could use the exercise. And strolling through Magnolia Harbor was a pleasure in any weather.

"Sure. I could use the fresh air." Dean put on a knitted wool cap and a peacoat. "We can have hot drinks by the fire when we get back."

"We'll need them," Charlotte said as they left his office. She waited while Dean told the receptionist where he was going, then allowed him to open the door for her. He was very courteous, which secretly thrilled her. It made her feel cherished.

They walked along the road toward town in silence, taking in the winter landscape. Whitecaps were kicking up on the lake, which was steel gray today under the heavy clouds. Now and then a ray of sun peeked through, gilding the waves.

Soon they reached the waterfront park. It was basically deserted except for a couple of dog walkers.

"Want to swing?" With a laugh, Charlotte trotted toward the playground area and plopped down in a swing.

Dean followed and took the adjacent swing.

The chains creaked as they worked their legs, sending the swings higher and higher. She loved that she could be playful with Dean. They spent a lot of their time together laughing.

Their arcs gradually slowed, and the swings came to a halt.

"That was fun." Charlotte was slightly breathless from the effort.

"So tell me about the retreat," Dean said. "I understand everyone's coming over tonight for dinner?"

"Yes, we are." Charlotte thought about the event, trying to decide how to summarize it. "Maya Channing, the instructor, is fantastic. She's helping us figure out our direction in life and how to get there. There's also plenty of self-care. We're getting makeovers later in the week."

Dean tipped his head, studying her face. "You don't need a makeover. You're beautiful the way you are."

Charlotte put a hand to her disheveled hair, laughing. She felt her cheeks heat, which was actually welcome out here in the cold. "Anyway, Grace and I already have our direction, but it's nice to affirm it."

Dean's gaze rested on the lake. "It's kind of interesting that we both ended up owning inns, don't you think? A big change from a fast-paced restaurant environment."

"I don't miss that," Charlotte said. Then she amended her statement. "Well, maybe a little. It was exciting." And so it had been. But it was an excitement tinged with fear. The relentless pressure to produce new, exciting dishes felt like perching on a pinnacle in danger of toppling at any second. And now she had free creative reign in her own kitchen. No investors or managers to cramp her style.

"You're lucky you have Grace to help you," Dean said. "I'm doing both sides, kitchen and lodging. But at least it keeps me out of trouble."

Charlotte tried to imagine running the inn alone and failed. She needed Grace, not only for the physical labor but the moral support. "I am lucky, especially since we're on the same page with everything."

"Doing anything interesting lately?" he asked.

Coming from Dean, Charlotte knew this question was about recipes, not extracurricular activities. She loved sharing ideas with another chef, especially one as talented as Dean.

"We did individual hot pots today." Charlotte explained how each diner had added her choice of meat, vegetables, and starches to the soup. "They loved it." She took her phone out of her pocket and brought up the restaurant supply listing for the hot pots to show him.

"What a great idea," Dean said, scanning the listing. "I might add that to the menu this winter." He made a few suggestions for ingredients.

Charlotte chimed in with ideas for different combinations of meats, seafood, and vegetables. "Once you have the pots, you can make all kinds of dishes. I'm thinking about doing shrimp, pork, and beef dumplings."

"Talk about comfort food." Dean slid off the swing.

Charlotte got up too, and the pair started walking back toward The Tidewater. He told Charlotte about the new potato dishes he was making for winter, including the one for tonight's dinner.

The air was even colder now, and Charlotte was grateful when they reached the front door. "I can't wait for a hot drink," she said, preceding him into the lobby.

"How about hot chocolate?" Dean suggested. "I have a very decadent recipe, and I want you to tell me what you think of it."

Charlotte didn't know what thrilled her more—the prospect of drinking hot chocolate with Dean by a warm fire or that he wanted her opinion.

Both were pretty sweet in her eyes.

9

April

April hadn't gone shopping for clothes in ages. Ever since her diagnosis, she'd avoided dress shops and swathed herself in sensible, comfortable outfits that were more suitable to a woman twice her age. And now, as she and her friends stood outside Miss Millie's, she was strangely reluctant to enter the boutique.

No, she was downright afraid.

Afraid to expose her body to the unflattering glare of a fitting room mirror, yes. That had never been enjoyable, even at her most trim and fit. But the fear rooting her feet to the sidewalk was related to something deeper.

Buying pretty clothes to adorn one's self was an act of faith and hope. Faith in one's own beauty and hope that this beauty would be seen.

April had lost both. She felt like an empty shell of a woman, defined more by her illness than any other attributes. She feared that no one would find her beautiful now. And facing that truth was devastating.

Jamie and Shelby walked through the boutique's front door.

Dawn tugged on April's arm, drawing her aside. "Are you all right?" she asked, her voice low. "If you don't feel like shopping, we can go get a coffee or something."

The offer was tempting. April bit her lip as she studied the dresses in the window. It would be so easy to bow out, to put off this hurdle for a little longer.

Then a flare of anger ignited in her core, mingled with fury at her cowardice and at an illness that had already taken so much. Surprising herself, she said, "No, let's go in. Maybe you can help me pick out a new outfit." April didn't trust her own judgment right now.

Dawn put her arm around April and grinned. "I'd love to. My daughter is gone, so I need someone else to focus on." One of Dawn's favorite activities was shopping with Abigail, but that rarely happened now that her daughter had moved away.

When they entered the store, Shelby and Jamie were already leafing through the racks of clothes.

A woman behind the counter smiled at the newcomers. "Welcome to Miss Millie's. I'm Sophie Mah. Please let me know if I can assist you."

"We will," Dawn said, steering April over to the dresses. "You need to find a nice dress, and I don't mean to wear to church. Something eye-popping. But elegant."

"I'm glad you added the elegant part," April said with a laugh. "I've never been eye-popping in my life." She actually preferred not to stand out in a crowd. Even more so now.

Dawn put both hands on April's shoulders and studied her, as if she'd never seen her before. "What are you talking about? You're gorgeous."

April snorted. "You only think that because you love me."

Her friend waved off the comment and flipped through the rack. "You're what, an eight?"

"A six," April admitted. Her treatments and the resulting nausea had made her drop more than ten pounds.

"Now I really hate you," Dawn teased. She pulled out several dresses and piled them into April's arms. "Here. Try these on."

April obeyed, ferrying the dresses to one of the changing rooms. She hung up the garments and pulled the brocade curtains closed. She kicked off her ankle boots, then without glancing in the mirror, she changed into the first dress. Made of a pink and silky jacquard fabric, it featured elbow-length kimono sleeves and a wraparound construction.

The size was right, but April still didn't peek at her reflection as she tied the sash. She squeezed her eyes shut, then slowly opened them.

The dress draped beautifully, flattering her shape, and the color suited her chestnut hair and pale complexion. Dawn was a genius.

"How are you doing in there?" Dawn asked.

April smiled. "I'm fine. Want to see?" She boldly opened the curtain and stepped out, not caring that she wore thick socks. "What do you think?"

"You look great," Shelby said.

Jamie whistled. "Whoa. That dress is gorgeous on you."

"Isn't it?" Dawn said, her voice full of pride. "How about the others I found? Do you like them?"

April regarded herself in a three-way mirror, tweaking the skirt into place. "I haven't tried them on. And I think this one is perfect."

Dawn straightened April's shoulder seam. "If you're on a roll, I say keep going."

Jamie held up several hangers. "That's my story, and I'm sticking to it." She bustled to another changing room. "Mama hasn't bought a new dress in over a year."

"Can you help me?" Shelby asked Dawn and Sophie. "I'm having a hard time finding anything that works for me because I'm so short and plump."

"We have something that will suit you." Sophie came out from behind the counter. "You have gorgeous skin and great curves, so we'll get you sorted out in no time."

As the shop owner conferred with Dawn and Shelby, April slipped into the changing room. She might as well try on the other dresses. It seemed her friends were going to be here a little longer.

In the end, she decided to buy a skirt and top in fine green wool with rust accents. She could wear the outfit for parent meeting days and special events.

After changing back into her regular clothes, April stepped into the main shop.

Jamie was admiring her reflection in a flowing silk dress, and Shelby was talking to Sophie about a blue-and-green wrap dress that flattered her figure.

"You both look beautiful," April said. "Where's Dawn?"

"In here," came the muffled reply. The curtain swept back, and Dawn walked out. She wore a fitted sheath in dove gray with a bolero jacket. With her slim build and mile-long legs, she was stunning.

"Wow," April said. "You should wear a dress more often." Dawn usually dressed in pants and tops, sophisticated but casual.

Dawn cocked a finger and pointed at April. "Right back at you." She whirled around. "This ought to knock Jim's eyes out when I wear it for our anniversary next month."

"He'll fall in love all over again," Jamie agreed.

While waiting for Dawn to try on other outfits, April and Jamie perused the jewelry. They both picked out new earrings.

Shelby stood in a corner of the store, folding sweaters another pair of customers had left in a jumbled heap.

Sophie went over to Shelby. "You don't have to do that," she said with a laugh.

"Why not? I love organizing." Shelby's folding was expert and fast.

As she pitched in, Sophie said, "You should do it as a business."

Shelby paused and glanced at her. "Guess what? I was just thinking about doing that."

"You should seriously consider it. I love owning a small business." Sophie began telling Shelby her story and giving her advice.

Dawn emerged from the fitting room. "My credit card will take a hit, but I'm buying all this." She set several outfits on the counter. "I don't think I bought a thing while my daughter was in college."

"Moms are like that. All sacrifice." Jamie held up a pair of dangly earrings studded with tiny gems. "What do you think?"

"Just right with that dress," Dawn said. She began turning the earring stand. "I could use some new jewelry too."

The foursome finally stumbled out of Miss Millie's, burdened with bags. They were a little poorer but a whole lot happier.

A gust of wind hit April right in the face. "Should we get coffee before we go back to the inn?"

Dawn checked her phone. "We have time, so let's do it. Then our last stop will be Spool & Thread. I want to pick up an embroidery kit."

They strolled down the street, greeted by friendly smiles from other people on the sidewalk.

"This is such a cute town," Shelby said. "I love it."

The Dragonfly Coffee Shop was noisy with chatter and the clatter of dishes. Although the shop was busy, the women found a table in the corner and dropped their purchases, then went to the counter.

Angel emerged from the back room. "Hello. How is your day going?" She smoothed her apron, prepared to wait on them.

"We enjoyed a little retail therapy, and now it's break time," Dawn said. "Why are you working? I thought you said you had the day off."

Angel shrugged. "One of the other baristas is sick, so I told my boss I could work a couple of hours. But I'll be at the inn this evening."

"I hope he appreciates your loyalty," Jamie said.

"Don't worry. He owes me one." Angel grinned. "So, what can I get you?"

They ordered cappuccinos and chai tea and carried the cups over to their table. Jamie lingered to talk to Angel about being an artist. Making a living from her work was Angel's North Star goal.

"Angel is a fantastic connection," Jamie said when she joined them at the table. "She knows the best shows to attend in the South."

"That's great," Shelby said, but she sounded distracted. "Do you think it's a sign?"

"What do you mean?" April asked.

"Sophie mentioning an organizing business," Shelby answered.

"It confirms that you've got a timely idea," Dawn said.

"That always happens to me," Jamie said. "Once I decide to do something, it seems to pop out at me everywhere."

April set her cup of tea down and smiled at Shelby. "It's timely, and you have talent. Sounds like a winning combination."

"So I should do it?" Shelby asked. She cleared her throat and repeated it, making it a statement. "I should do it. I will do it. I will start a business."

The three friends smiled at one another, recognizing they were seeing Shelby's transformation before their very eyes. She was moving from trepidation to determination.

April wanted some of that for herself. Buying pretty outfits was certainly a boost, but she had yet to dip her toe into the dating world again. But watching her friends laugh and chat, she realized she didn't have to worry about that right now.

It was enough to sit back and enjoy the moment.

10

Shelby

Shelby felt lit up. It was as if a light bulb had turned on in her heart and brain. She sat quietly with her cappuccino, listening to Jamie and Dawn banter. They were so funny. She could tell they had been friends for a long time by the way they teased each other.

The Miss Millie's shopping bag nudged her leg when she shifted in her seat. What a beautiful dress. *If only Devon . . .* Shelby shut down that line of thought. She'd been doing so well today, as if the change in scene had also made her broken heart seem distant as well.

Back to that light bulb. Shelby took a pen and a small notebook out of her handbag. She decided to jot down notes about her business idea whenever they struck. Then she would work on a business plan. She wrote a few ideas about customers. She'd been thinking mainly about working for individuals in their homes. But what about offices or retail? Someone like Sophie was already stretched thin. And retail stores needed to be changed each season to stay fresh and enticing.

"Getting some good ideas?" April asked.

Shelby glanced up. Jamie and Dawn were on their way to the restroom, so it was only her and April at the table. "I am," she said, setting her pen on the table. "I've learned to write things down when they come to me."

"Me too," April said, her expression sheepish. "My mind is a sieve some days."

Shelby regarded her new friend, sensing the sadness behind her cheerful expression. Once again, she experienced a pang of regret at taking her life so seriously. "I'm not going to waste another minute on Devon," she announced.

April's eyes widened. "Devon Miller?"

Shelby winced. She hadn't meant to say his name. Sievelike mind or not, April had connected the dots. But then the dam holding back her hurt released. Maybe it would help to talk about it. "Yeah. We dated for a few months, but it didn't work out."

April's gaze rested on her, but it felt comforting, not intrusive. "I'm sorry to hear that. It was recent, I'm guessing."

"Last week," Shelby told her. "But I'm starting to get over it."

"You will," April said. "Try not to beat yourself up. It can take a while, but you'll get there. Be patient with your heart."

"Thanks," Shelby said. "I needed to hear that."

Jamie and Dawn returned to the table.

"Ready, girls?" Dawn asked. "I still want to stop by the fabric shop."

Even after a lengthy browse in Spool & Thread, the group returned to the inn with plenty of time to rest before the next session. They were greeted by Winston when they walked through the door.

Up in her room, Shelby hung her new dress in the closet, admiring it once again. She couldn't wait to wear it.

Her phone rang, making her treacherous heart leap. But it was her mother. "Hey, Mom," she said, collapsing onto the soft bed. "How's everything?"

Her mother went on about the weather and Shelby's dad and their dog for a few minutes, giving her daughter the full update. Then she asked, "How's the retreat?"

Shelby glanced around the Wisteria Loft Suite. "It's wonderful. I have the prettiest room. It's on the third floor of a beautiful antebellum mansion."

"It sounds like a nice place," Mom said. "Maybe your dad and I will plan a trip there."

"You should. There are lots of nice shops in town too." Shelby told her about the new dress.

"It sounds lovely," her mother said. She paused. "You know how we watch the local news at lunchtime?"

"Yes," Shelby said slowly, her shoulders tensing. She remembered the ritual well. Her dad owned a car repair business on the same property as their house, and her mom helped in the office.

"So, there was a feature about the races coming up, and they interviewed Devon." Mom paused once more, then added in a hesitant voice, "He was with a blonde woman."

Shelby squeezed her eyes shut, humiliated once again. "Yeah, he's dating someone else."

"What was that?" Mom asked, raising her voice. There was a loud clanging in the background. "Hold on." She must have shut a door because the noise stopped.

Don't make me repeat it. "Devon and I broke up," she mumbled. That would work, act like it was her idea. It meant acknowledging her mother's reservations, but at this point, that was less painful than the truth.

"Good," her mom said. "Oh, I'm sorry. That just popped out. I never felt he was right for you."

"I know," Shelby said, then changed the subject. "I have big news. I'm going to start my own business."

"What are you talking about? Bookkeeping?"

Shelby caught a glimpse of her annoyed expression in the

dresser mirror and forced a smile. "Nope. Organizing. Like on that television show."

A long silence. "You're going to quit your job?" Her mom sounded scandalized by the idea.

"Dad's an entrepreneur," Shelby reminded her. Maybe his example had rubbed off on her.

She could practically feel her mother searching for a comeback. "True, but he worked for someone else for ten years first. Learned the ropes. Built up a loyal customer base."

"Well, there aren't any organizing companies that I can work for. So I need to build my business from scratch." When Shelby said it like that, she had to admit it did sound daunting. "I might be able to do accounting part-time while I start up, though."

Mom sighed. "Be careful, okay? Make sure you look before you leap."

Shelby bit back irritation with an effort. She knew her mother meant well, but Shelby had been nothing but careful all her life. The riskiest thing she had done so far was say yes to a date with a charismatic young driver.

And look where that got you. Shelby nearly groaned, hearing her mother's voice in those admonishing words. She took a deep breath before speaking. "I've got to go. We'll discuss it when I get home."

Her mom made a huffing sound but gave in. "All right. Have a good time."

Shelby tossed the phone facedown onto the bed. She should have known better than to broach the topic of starting a business over the phone and before it was fully thought out.

Then she laughed as she thought of a silver lining. At the very least, her mother's doubts would push her to create a bulletproof business plan.

She just had to keep the doubts out of her head.

April

"Do you want to ride with us to The Tidewater?" Dawn asked Shelby, who was walking down the stairs to the inn lobby. "We have room."

Shelby appeared lost in thought. "Yes, I'd like that. Thanks." She frowned. "Sorry. I had a phone call earlier, and it's still bugging me."

April wondered if Devon was the caller, but she didn't ask. If Shelby wanted to talk about it, she'd get there in her own time.

The women went out the front door. April was the last to exit, walking slowly due to stiff muscles. After the sharing session, Maya had led them through a very energetic jazz dance lesson.

"That was quite a workout this afternoon, wasn't it?" April said when she noticed Shelby waiting for her in the drive. "I guess I'm really out of shape."

"No, it was tough. Harder than I expected." Shelby hesitated, then said, "Did Maya seem different to you this afternoon?"

April recalled the sharing session. It had been cut short when Maya received a phone call. When she came back, she had started the exercise routine right away rather than let the last few people speak. "Maybe something's going on that we don't know about." It must be hard to be a motivational speaker. What did they do when they felt unmotivated themselves? Surely no one could be upbeat and positive every single day of the year.

"Yeah, we need to cut her some slack," Shelby said. "She can't hold us all up every second." She opened one of the car's rear doors.

"I call shotgun," Jamie said with a laugh, climbing into the front passenger seat.

"Be that way," April retorted, not miffed in the least. As she went around to the other rear door, she reflected on Shelby's words, thinking they were quite profound. Leaders were often expected to have almost superhuman strength and resilience.

She ought to know. Teachers were treated the same way. All those lovely children looking up to her, depending on her to guide them, teach them, and keep them safe. What a huge responsibility.

Before April had gone on leave for treatments, she had struggled to keep it together. When one of the children started crying, she'd wanted to burst into tears herself. She had often been preoccupied, a real no-no when working with kids.

So when she returned to the classroom, she needed to be in tip-top shape, mentally and emotionally. Her little guys and gals deserved her best.

The route to The Tidewater took them to the other side of the lake. The parking lot was fairly full. April thought that was a good sign. She idly wondered if most of the customers were local. Did Magnolia Harbor get any visitors at this time of year?

Dawn parked beside a truck with North Carolina plates, which answered April's question about visitors.

A welcome gust of warmth greeted them when they stepped inside the building.

"Good evening," the pleasant hostess said. "How many?"

"We're with the Magnolia Harbor Inn party," Dawn said.

The hostess nodded. "Right this way." She gathered four menus and led them to the dining room.

As they walked past the staircase, two men came down, one in his fifties and one about thirty.

Since they were on a collision course, the older man halted and stood back to let them pass. "Evening, ladies."

April's gaze caught his, and she smiled, realizing with a start how good-looking he was. He had thick gray hair, a gray goatee, and sparkling blue eyes.

"I'll be right with you, Mr. Philbrick," the hostess said. "After I seat these guests."

"Take your time," Mr. Philbrick replied. Turning to April, he made a tiny bow and smiled. "Have a good evening."

April nodded and scooted ahead, her cheeks flaming. How embarrassing. He'd caught her staring.

The four friends were first to arrive, and the hostess seated them near the fireplace. "How's this?"

"Perfect," Dawn said, sitting down in the end seat. She picked up the pitcher of water already on the table and started filling glasses for the others.

April took a chair next to Dawn, and Jamie and Shelby sat across from them.

April picked up the menu to peruse the entrées. Each one sounded more delicious than the last.

"There goes my diet," Jamie remarked as she scanned the menu. "I'm torn between the blackened salmon and the steak tips."

"Be sure to save some room," Dawn said. "I heard the desserts are excellent."

"I'll bet everything is," Shelby added. "Dean Bradley is a renowned chef, according to his bio. And he used to work at Le Crabe Fou in Charleston."

"Oh, lucky us," April said, studying the menu with even more interest.

"Remember how Charlotte was telling us about her job at Le Crabe Fou?" Dawn asked. "I wonder if she worked with Dean there."

"Maybe so," Jamie said.

The hostess reentered the dining room to seat the two men from the lobby. She put them at a table right next to April and her friends.

When April peeked over, once again she met Mr. Philbrick's eyes. And once again, he smiled.

A few minutes later, a few familiar women crowded through the dining room doorway and were guided to April's table by the hostess.

Paisley pulled out a chair beside April. "Fancy meeting you here."

"Glad you could make it," April said with a laugh. After a couple of days with these women, they were starting to feel like friends.

"My husband, Bryson, insisted I come." Paisley flapped her napkin open and settled it on her lap. "Between school and family, I don't get many nights out."

"I hear you," April said. Even though she didn't have a husband or kids—yet, she reminded herself—her calendar was often too packed for fun. Sometimes she even had to schedule getting together with Jamie and Dawn. She said as much to Paisley.

"It seems like I have homework myself every night, just to stay on top of the requirements," Paisley said.

"I know what you mean." April listened as Paisley discussed the latest round of testing her school was doing.

"Where's Maya?" Dawn asked, motioning to the only empty chair remaining at the table.

"She said she wasn't feeling well," Winnie replied.

"I hope she doesn't have Spencer's flu," Grace said. "He's pretty sick."

"Was he doing any better this afternoon?" Winnie asked.

Grace fiddled with her silverware. "Thankfully, yes. Charlotte's soup did the trick. At least that's what he said."

Charlotte laughed. "Yes, my magic chicken broth to the rescue."

April once again recalled Maya's phone call during class. She thought the speaker was more likely to be dealing with a personal crisis rather than a physical illness. Or maybe a business problem. Those could be consuming as well.

A tall, handsome man in chef's whites approached their table. April assumed he was Dean Bradley. He spoke to Charlotte for a few minutes, and it appeared they knew each other well.

"They're dating," Paisley whispered behind her hand.

April studied the pair, both attractive and talented chefs too. "Wow. Dynamic duo."

"I'll say." Paisley smiled. "They started out as rivals. Worked at the same restaurant in Charleston."

"Le Crabe Fou?" April asked.

Paisley nodded. "Now they both own inns in Magnolia Harbor. It was meant to be."

April loved hearing this real-life romantic tale, but she had to admit a stab of envy. Where was her soul mate? Why had she never met him?

Charlotte tapped a spoon on a glass. "Everyone, for those who don't know him yet, this is Chef Dean Bradley, our host tonight."

The ladies clapped, as did the other diners nearby.

April sneaked a glance at Mr. Philbrick. Yes, he was clapping too.

"Good evening," Dean said, his voice deep and resonant. "Welcome to The Tidewater. Tonight we have some very special dishes for you. We have crispy-skin duck confit, herb-crusted rack of lamb, and a mushroom risotto that seems to be the favorite tonight. Personally, I like the whipped butternut squash that comes with the duck. Your server will be back to take your orders in a moment. I hope you enjoy the meal." He smiled around the table, pecked Charlotte on the cheek, and strode over to another group of diners.

Jamie propped her chin on her hand, watching Dean walk away. "I'll eat anything that man cooks."

Charlotte laughed. "Don't let him hear you say that. His head is big enough." But her laugh said otherwise. She was beaming with sheer happiness.

The server returned with beverages and took their dinner orders. April decided on the stuffed sea bass. She loved seafood, but she lived so far inland that she rarely ate it.

As they waited for their food, April continued to chat with Paisley about teaching and other topics of mutual interest. April was thankful Paisley didn't pry into her personal life. The topic of cancer didn't come up either, and although her illness always hovered like a shadowy ghost, April didn't pay it any mind.

"Sea bass with garlic mashed potatoes?" a server said nearby.

Assuming that was her order, April turned in her seat.

But the young woman, not the one who took their order, was setting the plate down in front of Mr. Philbrick.

He put up both hands. "Sorry, ma'am. But that's not mine. Trevor and I have seen enough bass this week."

"That's right," his companion said. "We've been fishing every day. Even in the snow."

The server stood back, obviously flustered. "Oh, I'm sorry. Wrong table."

"I had the sea bass," April said.

"And I suppose you didn't have the salmon?" the server asked Trevor.

"No, ma'am," the young man said. "Dad and I both ordered the steak tips."

The server delivered the plate of sea bass to April, then glanced around and asked, "Salmon with garlic mashed potatoes?"

Paisley raised a hand. "That's mine." After the server deposited her plate, Paisley said to April, "I love mashed potatoes. When I have a rough day, it's just me and a big bowl of them." She took a scoop of butter from a dish. "And lots of butter."

April nodded as she added some butter to her potatoes. "That's the only way to eat them." After waiting for everyone to be served, she took a bite of the bass, which melted in her mouth. What a treat this was. Fire at her back, friends all around her, and delicious food.

Her spirits soared. *Thank You for all these blessings.*

Dean reappeared when they were finished with the entrées and the servers were clearing the plates. "Are you ready for dessert?"

He received groans and exclamations in response.

"You'll definitely want this dessert," Dean assured them.

"What does he mean?" April asked Paisley. "Is it something special he made for us?"

The chef overheard. "You might say that, but Charlotte actually made this."

The hostess glided into the dining room, a large, lit birthday cake in her hands.

At their table, Jamie covered her face with her hands. She moved them enough to peek at Dawn. "You didn't."

Dawn's expression was smug. "I did."

Jamie tended to downplay her birthday so much that April had even forgotten about it. "I'm so sorry," April said to her friend. "I didn't get you anything."

"Don't worry about it," Jamie said. "I have everything I need."

The hostess set the cake in front of Jamie, and everyone began to sing.

Jamie's face turned beet red at this attention, but when it was time, she managed to blow out all the candles at once. "Not bad for an old lady," she crowed.

Everyone laughed and broke into applause.

Jamie was far from old. April smiled, watching her friend chat with the others as she cut the cake, giving everyone a slice.

Then Jamie gestured to the next table. "You fellows want a piece? There's plenty."

April realized Jamie was talking to Mr. Philbrick and Trevor.

"Why, sure, if you have enough," Trevor said. "What do you think, Dad?"

Mr. Philbrick patted his lean belly. "Sure, I'll take a sliver. Thanks."

As Jamie cut their slices, Paisley got up. "Excuse me. I see someone I need to talk to." Carrying her cake, she wandered across the dining room to another table.

Charlotte had also wandered off, so there were two empty seats at the table. When the two men came to get their cake, April said, "Have a seat."

Trevor took Charlotte's seat next to Shelby.

Mr. Philbrick hesitated before sitting beside April. "Hi, I'm Owen," he said, holding out a hand.

"I'm April." She shook his hand, which was large and warm. "You're staying here at The Tidewater?" It was an easy guess, since he'd been coming down the stairs when they arrived.

"We are." Owen forked up a piece of cake and chewed. "Annual fishing trip. We live near Charlotte."

"Shelby's from Charlotte," April said. "I'm from Asheville, and so are my friends. This is Jamie and Dawn."

"Nice country up there," Owen said. "We like the mountains too. Fly-fishing in mountain brooks." His blue eyes glowed with remembered pleasure.

"I take it you like fishing," April said with a grin. Was that his filter for every location?

"I love being outside, with water and sky all around," Owen said. "It gives me a sense of perspective."

April could understand that. "Even in the winter?"

"Yes, but it's not usually this cold," Owen answered. "We basically had the lake to ourselves. Plus, the fish don't care. They still bite."

"It's been cold all right," April said. "It snowed the day we got here. So what do you do when you're not fishing?"

Owen motioned to the fireplace. "Sit by the fire with a good mystery novel."

"I love mysteries too," April said. She actually liked many genres, but she was glad to find common ground with this nice man.

As they discussed favorite authors, April realized she was enjoying herself. But he was probably married. Then she glanced at his left hand. No wedding ring. Maybe he was divorced.

Across the table, Trevor laughed at something Shelby had said.

Owen had at least one grown child. How much more baggage was he carrying? Then she scolded herself for running too far ahead. She'd barely met the man. Couldn't she simply chat with him over cake and leave it at that?

As Owen opened his phone to share his to-read list, April decided that she could. Tonight she would talk books and fishing and any other topic that arose. She was having a great time.

12

Grace

"Good morning, everyone," Maya called. "How did you sleep?" The instructor, clad in pale-pink leggings and a matching T-shirt, appeared tired, but her voice still had a galvanizing effect on the crowd.

Grace stood straighter. She noticed that everyone else did too.

Maya's question was answered with groans, exclamations, and affirmatives.

"The jazz class wore me out," Judith said. "I could hardly stay awake to eat that delicious dinner."

"Wasn't it wonderful?" Missy batted her thick, false eyelashes.

"I still can't get over how you surprised me with a birthday cake," Jamie said. "But remember, to everyone else, I'm still thirty-nine." She made a shushing sound, finger to her lips.

The women laughed.

"Thirty-nine forever," Dawn called.

"Count me in," Winnie shot back. "I've been thirty-nine for more than twenty years."

Laughter greeted this remark as well.

"Thirty-nine forever," Maya mused. "That could be our motto. Young enough to set the world on fire but old enough to know what you're doing."

Grace was almost fifty, and although she was tired some days, in general she didn't think about her age. It was a far cry from when she was young and thought anyone over forty would spend their time in a rocking chair. Ah, the ignorance of youth. When her husband was killed in a train crash more than twenty years ago, she'd gleaned a lasting lesson. Life was a gift, and she should make the most of it. Glancing around the room, noticing how her guests were listening with rapt attention to Maya, she had to admit that she was doing all right in that department. There wasn't anything else she would rather be doing.

"You're only as old as you think you are," Maya said.

"Tell that to my back," Judith retorted.

Maya chuckled in agreement, then went on. "When it comes to making life choices, that is. Many people are now embarking on two or even three careers. They're having families later and following dreams in midlife."

Grace was on her second career and had bought the inn at forty. So she was an example of two out of three. As for the family, she had already done that. But some days she thought she wouldn't mind dating. Maybe.

She wondered how Spencer was doing, if he felt better. Then she laughed at herself. It was interesting how thoughts of dating led to Spencer.

"This morning, we're going to do some gentle stretching," Maya said. "After breakfast, we'll get in our small groups again."

"Is the stretching gentle-gentle or Maya-gentle?" Jamie asked. She stretched out a leg with a groan. "I'm still stiff from yesterday's class."

Laughter and agreement followed this comment.

Maya laughed too. "I promise I'll take it easy on you." And she did, leading them through a series of slow exercises that made Grace feel quite limber.

When they finished, Charlotte called, "Breakfast in the dining room. Oatmeal smorgasbord."

The unusual dish got lots of remarks as the women headed toward the dining room in a pack.

The serving table held two urns with steaming hot oatmeal. The smorgasbord included nuts, fresh berries and apples, syrups, brown sugar, dried raisins and cranberries, skim milk, and cream. The guests exclaimed over the choices as they put together their bowls.

"What a great idea," Winnie said to Charlotte. "You really did a new take on a classic breakfast."

"I hope so," Charlotte said. "Oatmeal is good for you, and there are so many ways to enjoy it."

When the guests were finished at the buffet table, the ladies of the inn served themselves. Grace chose raspberries, maple syrup, and cream to top her oatmeal. Along with a big mug of coffee, this breakfast would fuel her for the day.

After breakfast, while the guests chatted at the table, Grace helped Charlotte and Winnie clean up. They put away leftover toppings and loaded the dishwasher, set out fresh urns of coffee and hot water, then joined the others for the small group discussion.

But before she went into the other room, Grace texted Spencer. *How are you today? Let me know if you need anything.* That was less intrusive than calling, especially if he was sleeping.

But the answer came right back. *Much better. Thanks again for your help.*

She was glad that he was on the mend.

In the living room, Maya had divided the attendees into groups. "Grace," she said, "I want you to be in this group." She led Grace to where April and her friends were seated.

"Hi again," Grace said, taking a seat on the sofa next to Shelby. "Are you enjoying the retreat?" She welcomed the chance to get feedback for future events.

"We love it," Jamie said. "Don't we, girls?"

They all agreed.

"We've made so much progress in such a short time," Dawn said. "It's hard to believe."

Maya addressed the room. "I'm glad to hear it, Dawn. Today we're going to talk about shifting priorities. When we set our sights on a major goal, we often have to change something in our everyday lives. Add some things, eliminate others. If we don't, then we'll find ourselves doing the same old thing, and our goal will slip into the background. Today, decide what you're going to shift in your lives, so your goal can become one of your priorities."

The room broke into excited chatter.

"That makes total sense," Jamie said. "With each baby, I had to make time for exercise, to get back in shape." She laughed. "And that was a challenge. Good thing my hubby is a hands-on parent."

Grace smiled as she imagined the happy chaos at Jamie's house with half a dozen children running around.

"My husband helped a lot too," Dawn said. "Although we had only one daughter."

Grace glanced around the circle. "Who wants to go first? I'm already living my North Star goal, but I'm anxious to hear about yours."

Shelby shifted on the sofa cushion. "I guess I will." She swallowed visibly. "You won't jump on me, I hope."

"Of course not," Jamie said. "This is a safe space."

The young woman clasped her hands in her lap, staring down at her intertwined fingers. "As I mentioned the other day, my North Star goal is to start an organizing business."

"Oh, that's a great idea," Grace said. "We could have used an organizer when setting up the inn. We were overwhelmed with things to do."

Shelby nodded. "Everyone I talk to thinks it's a good move. Well, except my mother. She's worried about me giving up the security of my job." She swallowed again. "Which does pay well. I'll need a lot of clients to make up for my current salary and benefits."

Having been through the business start-up phase, Grace had some wisdom to impart. "Before you do anything, figure out the numbers. What you need to earn, what you think you'll earn, and how many clients you'll need."

"It'll help you make the case to your mom," Dawn said. "She's just being a mom."

"When Charlotte and I bought the inn, we plunged in full-time," Grace said. "Do you think you'll be able to do that too?"

Shelby shook her head. "I was thinking I could work in accounting part-time. Then when I build up enough clients, I'll let that go."

The others applauded her plan of action.

"What's the priority you need to set right now?" Grace asked. "As the first step."

Shelby picked up her pen. "Figure out the finances for my business." She wrote something else. "I'll commit to working on that for an hour a day instead of surfing social media."

"That's wonderful advice," Jamie said to Grace. "We don't have to do the whole thing at once. We can take one step at a time."

After Shelby, Jamie discussed how she was going to fit time to paint into her busy schedule. Most of the kids were in school, but she still had two at home.

"Write it on the calendar, and tell the family it's not negotiable," Dawn advised. "Well, unless someone breaks a bone or sets the kitchen on fire."

"If my husband can't watch the kids, then I'll get a babysitter at the house," Jamie said. "He or she can put out fires, real or imaginary. Once I get painting, I'm in my own world."

When it came to Dawn's priority, she had to take her own advice.

"I'll write in the mornings before I go to the library. And at lunch when I can."

"You'll achieve your goal," Jamie said. "A few words at a time."

Dawn made some calculations on her notepad. "I should be able to finish a book in six months. That's not bad."

April was last. A blush suffused her pale skin. "I realized something huge last night," she said in a soft voice. "I keep thinking something magical will happen and I'll meet Mr. Right. But I need to put myself out there."

"Yeah, we noticed you chatting with Owen last night," Jamie said, grinning. "Is he single?"

"He's a widower. He has three sons." She glanced at Shelby, who suddenly got busy with her pen. "Trevor is the youngest."

"So what do you think is your priority?" Grace asked. She checked her phone. Time was almost up, but she didn't want to rush April. She searched for Maya, thinking they could extend the session, but the instructor wasn't in the room.

"I need to go somewhere once a week," April said. "A place where I can meet people. Sitting at home watching a movie won't get me a date."

"You could try online dating," Dawn suggested.

April shuddered. "No thanks. I'm going to do it the old-fashioned way. Through making friends."

"That's a good approach," Grace said. "It makes it easier to vet people."

Charlotte appeared at her side, bending down to whisper, "Winnie needs to talk to you."

Grace set aside her pad of paper and pen. "Please excuse me, ladies. Continue on."

She and Charlotte crossed the room, meeting Winnie in the doorway. They walked into the foyer.

"What's going on?" Grace asked, making sure they were out of earshot.

"About half an hour ago, I saw Maya heading upstairs. She was crying." Winnie frowned. "I think something's seriously wrong."

Grace did as well. A professional like Maya wouldn't normally run off from a session in progress. "I'll go check on her."

"I'll go with you," Winnie said.

Charlotte nodded. "I'll have the women take a coffee break and put out some cookies and fruit."

"Thanks," Grace said. She and Winnie climbed the stairs to the second floor. "I've had the feeling for a while that something is troubling Maya," she whispered to Winnie.

"Me too," Winnie said. "Starting when she was late. I thought it might be more than the weather causing a delay."

They paused outside the Dogwood Suite. Grace rapped on the door. When Maya didn't answer, she knocked again. "Maybe she's asleep," Grace said to her aunt.

Winnie sucked in air. "I hope not. What are we going to do with the class?"

But then a wan voice called through the door, "Hello? Is someone out there?"

"Yes, Maya. It's me, Grace. And Winnie. We wanted to check on you."

A long silence followed. "I'm sorry," Maya finally said. "I can't come down right now."

13

Charlotte

In the kitchen, Charlotte arranged three kinds of homemade cookies on a tray—chocolate chip, peanut butter, and oatmeal. The classics. Then she put on a fresh pot of coffee, having checked the urn, which was low.

All the while she hoped that everything was all right with Maya. She'd never been to a conference where the speaker left suddenly. But that was life. She had every confidence that Grace and Winnie would figure it out, and Charlotte would help however she could.

She was about to deliver the tray of cookies when her phone went off. A text from Dean. *Matinee this afternoon? Classic noir festival.*

The answer to that was simple. After lunch, the retreat schedule included a free afternoon. As for social hour, Charlotte had already prepared the food, and it was in the fridge, ready to serve. She wrote back that she'd love to go. Dean offered to pick her up at one. His sous-chef would run the kitchen while he took a well-deserved break.

With a lighter heart, she picked up the tray of cookies and headed to the dining room. "Coffee break," she sang out. "Three kinds of homemade cookies."

"I'll take one of each," Jamie declared, hopping out of her chair.

With talking and laughter, the women took their break.

Charlotte was relieved that no one asked about the instructor. As Charlotte kept an eye on the proceedings, she glanced at the door, hoping Maya would show up.

Grace peeked into the room and gestured for Charlotte to step out into the foyer, where Winnie was also waiting.

"What's going on?" Charlotte whispered.

"Maya is too upset to teach." Her sister crossed her arms. "I guess I'll be taking her place."

"Can't we just end the session right now?" Charlotte asked. "Everyone seems to be in a good mood."

The lively voices drifting in from the other room confirmed her statement.

"I hate to deviate from the agenda," Grace said. "Besides, they get a lot out of the sharing session."

Charlotte was thinking more about her date with Dean, but she nodded. "Go ahead. I'm sure it will be fine."

"I'm not," Grace said with a sigh. "Okay, wish me luck." She walked into the dining room.

"I'm not trying to be nosy, but what's going on with Maya?" Charlotte asked. "I'm curious."

Winnie pressed her lips together. "I don't know very much. After she told us she couldn't finish today's session, she mentioned her husband. I'm pretty sure she's having marital problems."

Charlotte's heart panged with sympathetic sorrow for Maya. "That's tough. Especially when she's supposed to be upbeat and positive."

"Exactly," Winnie said. "I think she feels she can't reveal any of her turmoil, and the weight of it finally broke her down."

"We'll have to pamper her." Charlotte put a hand on Winnie's shoulder. "Do you want to take her a tray of cookies with coffee? Maybe she won't eat them, but at least she'll know we care."

"Cookies can make a whole lot of things a little bit better," Winnie said. "Yes, I'll take up a tray."

Charlotte put together the tray, including a small vase with one lovely flower from Grace. Winnie carried the tray upstairs, Winston at her heels. She soon returned, without the dog, who had apparently stayed behind to bestow his special brand of comfort.

In the living room, Grace called out, "Hello, everyone. I'll be your leader for the rest of this session." She paused. "Maya isn't feeling well."

Exclamations of concern and dismay filled the room, but the attendees didn't probe into exactly what was wrong.

Grace took the floor and led them through the sharing session. Each woman discussed her new priority and how it related to her North Star goal.

Charlotte thought about her own life. For years, she had been focused on running the inn with Grace. She had dated now and then, but there hadn't been anything serious. And not that she was serious about Dean. But it already felt different from a casual dating relationship. Maybe because she'd known him so long. They had been colleagues first, then rivals, finally friends . . . She tuned back in to hear Grace addressing her.

"Charlotte, anything to add in our discussion of priorities? You juggle running the inn, cooking, and writing cookbooks. How do you handle everything?"

Charlotte wasn't exactly sure. And now she had an important relationship to add to the mix. Finally, she formulated a response. "Well, in my case, it's not too bad. All three things are related. I cook for our guests and use those recipes in my cookbooks. And when I need help, I get it from Grace and Winnie and outside caterers."

Grace nodded. "There's a lesson. Get help when you need it. None of us can do it all, no matter how driven or competent we are."

Charlotte wondered if that was part of Maya's stress. The instructor was probably handling her business alone. And if she was traveling around the country speaking, maybe that placed a strain on her marriage.

"Sorry to put you on the spot," Grace said to Charlotte after the meeting broke up. "I could tell your mind was elsewhere after I called on you."

Charlotte picked up the almost empty cookie tray. "That's okay. I was just thinking."

"About lunch?" Grace asked. "I'll help you make the sandwiches."

She didn't bother to explain that she'd actually been thinking about Dean. "Thanks. I'll take you up on that."

They went to the kitchen. While they were putting together platters of meat and cheese and vegetables, Charlotte said, "I'm going to the movies with Dean this afternoon."

"That sounds relaxing." Grace opened a package of Swiss cheese. "I'm going to curl up by the fire with a book and Winston."

"Perfect choice," Charlotte said. She glanced out the window at the sky, where dark clouds gathered. "Especially in this weather."

Winnie entered the room, pushing up her sleeves. "Here to help," she said.

"Just in time, as always." Charlotte pointed to the platters. "Those are ready to go."

Grace finished arranging the cheese. "What are you doing this afternoon, Winnie?"

Their aunt picked up two platters, one in each hand. "I'm going to do some piecing on a baby quilt." Winnie was a member of the local quilting group, The Busy Bees.

"Sounds wonderful," Grace said. "I'm reading, and Charlotte is going to the movies."

"Life and work balance, that's what it's all about." With that nugget of wisdom, Winnie left the room.

"But what if your work is your life?" Charlotte asked with a laugh.

Grace smiled. "You force yourself to take breaks. Have a good time with Dean, okay? And forget about the inn."

At exactly one o'clock, Dean's silver Acura pulled into the inn drive and rolled to a stop near the front steps.

Charlotte, who had been watching for him, buttoned her coat and hurried outside.

As was his custom, he got out and came around the side of the car. After a quick kiss of greeting, he opened her door.

"You're spoiling me," she said as she got in.

"You're worth it," Dean replied, shutting the door. Back at the wheel, he headed down the drive.

"Where are we going?" Charlotte asked. She hadn't bothered to ask him via text message.

He named a theater that specialized in independent and art films located in a nearby town. "They're doing a noir retrospective this week."

"Nice. What are we seeing?" She had a working knowledge of classic films, but Dean was a movie buff. From the first silent films to this year's blockbusters, he enjoyed them all.

"*Double Indemnity*," he said in a dramatic voice. "Starring Fred MacMurray and Barbara Stanwyck."

"Sounds intriguing," Charlotte said.

"A number of noir films came out in 1944 or around that time," Dean said. He shared interesting tidbits about the genre.

Charlotte settled back and listened, comfortable in the warm car. Outside the window, the winter countryside flashed by.

Soon they turned off the main road and entered a charming small town with brick storefronts and a square. Finding herself excited by the change in scene, she realized she needed to get out more often.

When she expressed that, Dean laughed. "Me too," he said, sliding into a parking space across from the theater. "Like you, I live at my job. But I'm not complaining. I love my work, and I feel very fortunate."

"So do I," she said.

Dean turned off the engine, then got out and opened the door for her.

As she took his arm to cross the street, she said softly, "Very fortunate indeed."

The historic theater had been extensively renovated, and it featured carved plaster and wall murals. After paying for their tickets, Dean stopped at the concession stand and ordered a big tub of popcorn and two drinks.

Dean and Charlotte settled in about halfway up the rows of folding red velvet seats.

He held out the tub of popcorn so she could grab a handful, then glanced around at the other patrons. "I'm glad they're getting customers. Otherwise, they wouldn't be able to stay open."

"That would be too bad." Charlotte snuggled closer to Dean and prepared to be swept away into another world.

It took a moment for Charlotte to come back to herself after the movie. She stood and stretched, scanning the hushed theater. Other patrons were making their way to the exits.

"What a wonderful film," Charlotte said. She wanted to buy a new dress so she could look as glamorous as Barbara Stanwyck.

Dean helped her put on her jacket. "It's one of my favorites." He slipped into his own coat. "Want to get a coffee? There's a good bakery down the street."

"Great idea." Charlotte wasn't in a hurry to return to the inn.

As they stepped out of the warm cocoon of the theater, she noticed that the skies had cleared. Sunshine glinted off puddles. "It rained while we were inside."

"I see that." Dean steered her around a puddle on the sidewalk, keeping his arm around her. "The bakery is right down there."

Charlotte saw a retro neon sign hanging over the sidewalk. The interior of the bakery was equally charming, with tiled floors and a long bakery case and counter. Little tables stood around the room. "There's a window seat."

"Why don't you grab it?" Dean said, then headed toward the counter.

Charlotte went over and put her coat on the back of a chair.

A few minutes later, they were seated with steaming Americano coffees and bar cookies. Dean had lemon curd, and Charlotte had raspberry.

"Want to share?" Charlotte picked up a knife and cut hers in half.

"Of course," Dean answered.

After they enjoyed—and gently critiqued—the coffee and pastries, Dean said, "I love that we have cooking in common."

Charlotte smiled. She realized that she smiled often around Dean. "Me too. Other people don't get the obsession. I'm like a sponge when it comes to learning about food and trying new dishes. Then creating my own take on them." It wouldn't be an exaggeration to say that her inspiration was global. She loved how influences from Asian, European, and South American dishes found their way into the mainstream.

"Exactly. You're a food artist." Dean scrolled through his phone. "Want to see my idea board?"

Charlotte felt her mouth drop open. Chefs normally guarded every spark of inspiration, not wanting another professional to steal their thunder. For Dean to share this was huge. It meant he trusted her.

"I'd love to." She scooted her chair closer and peered at the screen.

As he showed her photographs he had saved, a silly thought popped into her head. People talked about couples making beautiful music together. She and Dean made beautiful food. And the best part was, they got to share it with other people.

14

Shelby

After lunch, while they were all still at the table, Dawn said, as if sharing a secret, "I'm going to spend the afternoon writing."

"Way to go," Jamie said. "I'm planning to sketch out a painting."

Shelby supposed she could start her business plan today, but she really wanted to get outside and enjoy the fresh air. She glanced out the window. The clouds had lifted, and sunshine glittered on the lake. It was beautiful.

Seeming to read her mind, April said, "Want to take a walk, Shelby? I'd like to wander around downtown some more."

Grace overheard their discussion as she cleared the nearby place settings. "If you're feeling especially energetic, you can walk from here. Or drive down and park in town, then walk."

Shelby and April locked eyes.

"Let's drive," Shelby said. "It will give us more time to explore."

"Sounds like a plan." April stood, grabbing the empty sandwich plates. "Meet in ten minutes? I'd like to wash up first."

"Sounds good." Shelby pushed back from the table and gathered the drink glasses, destined for the bus pan. She also dashed upstairs to brush her hair and change into better walking shoes. Gloves and a hat went into her tote, as did her camera.

They met in the lobby, where Winnie was doing some filing behind the desk. "Have a nice time," the older woman said. "I highly recommend the bookstore."

"Maybe we'll check it out," Shelby said. "We didn't make it there the other day."

Outside the inn, April said, "The women who work here are wonderful. Winnie is especially interesting."

"What do you mean?" Shelby asked, digging out her car keys. She pushed the fob to unlock the doors.

"The day after I got here, she gave me some toe warmers. The kind you use during activities in the great outdoors." April opened the passenger side door. "I have no idea why."

Shelby considered the gift as she slid into the car. "I don't either. I mean, it's been cold, but we're not hiking or camping during the retreat."

April hugged herself. "Brrr. And I'm glad."

Downtown Magnolia Harbor was fairly quiet, and they easily found a spot in the public parking lot near the waterfront park. Out on the lake, a fishing boat chugged through the waves, and Shelby wondered briefly if Trevor and his father were on it.

As if reading her mind again, April said, "Trevor seemed like a nice guy."

Without discussion, they headed to the crosswalk and Main Street.

"He is," Shelby said. "We had fun." She thought back to her time with Trevor. He was a great storyteller and had kept her entertained with tall tales about his fishing adventures. Thankfully, he had treated her with the utmost respect, without a hint of flirting or innuendo. "He'd make a good friend."

April raised her brows. "A friend?"

They had crossed the road, and Shelby stopped on the sidewalk, groaning. "Yes. I'm not ready for anything else." She smiled at April. "And what about you? I noticed you and Owen chatting up a storm."

Shelby wondered if something besides the brisk wind was responsible for the way April's cheeks turned pink.

April pushed back a stray lock of hair, not meeting Shelby's eyes. "We have a few things in common."

"Like what?" Shelby asked, curious. They began strolling up a street that intersected with Main Street.

"Mystery novels. Gardening. Music."

"Fishing?" Shelby guessed.

April shook her head. "I'm afraid not. I never saw the appeal of sitting in a boat for hours and hours, waiting for a fish to do something."

"Trevor said it's really peaceful," Shelby commented. "A nice break from their hectic construction business, Philbrick & Sons."

They reached Main Street, which was paved in cobblestones. Antique streetlamps arched over the sidewalk, and the window boxes and urns were full of evergreen branches and other seasonal displays. Magnolia Harbor was charming, no doubt about it.

"They own a company?" April asked. "Owen didn't mention it. He only told me he was a builder."

Shelby shrugged. "Maybe he was being modest. Trevor said they're working on a high-end development outside Charlotte."

"That's interesting." April pointed down the street. "There's the bookstore. Want to check it out?"

"Sure." Shelby studied the storefront as they approached. The Book Cottage was such a cute name.

Bells jingled as they entered the store.

An older woman with a highlighted brown bob glanced up from behind the counter. "Welcome to The Book Cottage. I'm Blanche Townsend. Please let me know if I can help you find something."

"Where's the mystery section?" April asked. To Shelby, she said, "Owen gave me some recommendations."

Blanche pointed to the spot, and April ambled that way.

Shelby scanned the shop, not quite sure what she felt like reading, and noticed a bookcase of business titles. Maybe they had books on starting a business.

Shelby found several books that appeared useful and grabbed them. They were a business expense, right? Smiling to herself at taking this official first step, she carried them to the counter.

"Are you all set?" Blanche asked.

Shelby saw a selection of beautiful cards nearby. "Can I leave these books here? I want to check out the cards."

Blanche moved the books aside. "Of course. By the way, those were painted by Angel Diaz, a local artist. She has them printed."

"Oh, I know Angel," Shelby said with a smile. She went over and spun the rack, picking out the prettiest cards. She was going to write her new friends thank-you notes. Plus, she could include her contact information inside. She didn't want to lose touch with April, Dawn, and Jamie. The women of the inn and Maya deserved cards too.

She carried a stack of the cards back to the counter. Spotting April coming her way, she said, "Please ring these up first."

Blanche caught on, giving Shelby a wink. "No problem." Since they were all the same price, she keyed in the number and dollar amount, then slid all the cards into a bag.

April buzzed up to the counter with her arms full. "I found a bunch of books." She set them down with a sigh.

"Mysteries," Blanche said. "One of our best-selling genres."

"I'm especially glad we didn't walk now," April said. "Can you imagine carrying these back to the inn?"

"Where are you staying?" Blanche asked. She put Shelby's books into the bag with the cards.

"The Magnolia Harbor Inn," Shelby said. "We're here for a women's retreat."

"With Maya Channing?" Blanche asked. "Oh, you lucky ducks. I've heard she's wonderful."

Shelby glanced at April, unable to suppress the memory of Maya leaving the session that morning. But there was no way she would ever gossip about Maya and potentially hurt her. "She is wonderful. I'm going to start a business because of her and the new friends I made."

"Good for you." Blanche handed Shelby her purchases and began ringing April up. "Are you starting a business too?"

April bit her lower lip, her cheeks flushing again. "No, my goals are more personal. I'm a schoolteacher, like Paisley Russell. She's attending the retreat as well. Do you know her?"

"Of course I do. Winnie Bennett's daughter." Blanche rang up the books and told April the total. "Great gals."

While waiting, Shelby saw a flyer taped to the front of the counter. It advertised trivia night at the Dragonfly Coffee Shop that evening. It sounded like fun.

April picked up her purchases. "Want to drop off our books and walk around a little more? We've barely gotten any exercise."

"Good plan," Shelby said. They strolled back down the street, stopping at the Dragonfly for cups of coffee to go. The poster was in the window there too. "Would you like to play trivia tonight?" she asked April as they left the coffee shop.

"Maybe," April said. "I'm not really big on trivia games."

"But I'll bet you're great at them since you're a teacher," Shelby said.

April laughed. "You might be right. I have so many random facts stuffed in my head that it's scary."

They walked along in silence, taking in the street scene.

"Do you think my goal is crazy?" April asked out of the blue.

Shelby barked a laugh. "What? No. You want to find someone and maybe get married. Why would that be crazy?"

April bit her lip, a gesture Shelby now guessed was an expression of vulnerability and insecurity. "Because I'm old, I guess. Something

I read the other day said fewer people are getting married nowadays. And the older you are, the less likely it is."

Shelby studied her new friend. April was not only pretty, but she was kind and smart too. "Maybe that's true for some people but not you. You're amazing, and believe me, someone is going to see that."

"I hope you're right." April's laugh was shaky. "It's a little strange to admit you want something when you're not sure you can have it."

"Yeah, I understand." For a gloomy second, Shelby thought of Devon. The whole time they dated, it had felt like she'd accidentally caught a magical creature. She feared that if she made a wrong move, he'd vanish. And so he had, although she hadn't done anything wrong. No, she'd been the perfect girlfriend—agreeable, accommodating, always letting him have his way.

Shelby halted on the sidewalk. She'd been a pushover. "I get it now. No wonder Devon dumped me. I was such a mouse."

April stopped walking too. "What do you mean?"

"I didn't think I deserved him," Shelby explained. "And because I acted that way, he didn't value me." She shook her head. "It's so clear to me now. I thought it was because I wasn't glamorous enough. Well, that's still true."

"No, it's not," April said. "You're gorgeous."

"I'm glad you think so." Shelby allowed the compliment to warm her heart. Maybe if she felt attractive, other people would see her that way. It was worth a shot. She caught her reflection in a shopwindow and raised her head, squaring her shoulders and straightening her spine. That was better.

"Okay, girl," April said, obviously noticing her new posture. "Let's strut to the car." She copied Shelby's attitude and set off, walking like a runway model.

They both burst into giggles but kept it up all the way back to the park.

They were loading the bags into the trunk of Shelby's car when a motorboat buzzed over to the dock.

Shelby recognized the men operating the craft. She elbowed April. "Don't look now, but Owen and Trevor just arrived."

Of course April turned to see, and a moment later, she waved at the men. "Let's go talk to them." She picked up her cup of coffee and headed in that direction, still strutting.

Shelby laughed to herself and grabbed her own cup. She locked the car and hurried after her new friend.

When Trevor glanced up and smiled at her, Shelby felt a new determination. She wouldn't be a mouse anymore. The next guy she went out with would be as lucky to date her as vice versa. Right?

15

April

April's heart gave a leap when she saw Owen at the wheel of the motorboat. *Slow down.* She had only talked to the man once. Besides, they were both visitors to Magnolia Harbor. It wasn't like they would see each other after they left town.

Too bad. April told her treacherous brain to pipe down.

The boat engine sputtered to a halt.

"Catch anything?" April called out, treading across the dock boards. The wind caught her hair, tossing it.

Under the shadow of his cap, Owen's expression was disappointed. "It's too choppy out there. We had to cut it short."

The breeze off the lake crept down April's collar, and she shivered. "It's pretty cold too."

"That doesn't usually bother us," Owen said. "We dress in layers and search for sheltered spots to fish."

Trevor leaped out to tie off the boat. He approached Shelby, and they started talking.

Owen climbed out of the boat. "We've been docking at The Tidewater but thought we'd grab a late lunch in town. Maybe get a coffee too."

April lifted her cup. "I recommend the Dragonfly Coffee Shop. We stopped there after shopping at The Book Cottage."

"Is the bookstore any good?" Owen asked. "Might be fun to browse after lunch."

"They have a great selection." Between sips of the rapidly cooling coffee, April told him about the titles she had purchased. "A few of those were your recommendations."

"I remember." Owen smiled. "Let me know what you think."

April's pulse jumped up a notch. It sounded like he wanted to stay in touch. After all, it wasn't possible for her to read all those books before she went home.

Trevor and Shelby joined them, and Trevor said, "Shelby and I are going to trivia night at the Dragonfly tonight."

"How does that sound?" Owen asked April. "Want to tag along with them?"

As April had mentioned to Shelby, she really didn't care for trivia. But it was a chance to spend time with Owen. And her resolution was to go out more often. "Yes, I'd like that."

After making sure the boat was secure, the couples strode across the park, arranging a time to meet at the Dragonfly.

"Whoever gets there first can save a table," Trevor said.

They parted ways in front of the chamber of commerce building.

For a moment, April watched the two men, so similar in height and looks, stroll down the path. Owen laughed at something his son said. He was so friendly and good-humored. She liked how easy it was to be in his company.

"You can tell they're related by the way they walk," Shelby said.

April agreed. She tore her gaze away from Owen and Trevor and tossed her empty coffee cup into a trash can. "What should we do now? Walk along the shore? I see there's a path."

Before Shelby could reply, the door to the chamber of commerce opened and someone called, "Hello, ladies."

April turned and saw the director poking her head out the door.

"Want to come in for coffee?" Missy asked them.

April and Shelby glanced at each other.

"Sure," April said. She'd seen Missy at the retreat but hadn't talked to her. This might be an opportunity to make another new friend.

As they approached the door, April admired the quaint building. It appeared to be a former train station. The structure was painted pale yellow and green, and it had overhanging eaves and a wide porch.

"Sorry for the mess," Missy said when they entered the main office. Stacks of brochures, booklets, posters, and assorted promotional items were scattered all over the room. "I decided to clean out the closets, and there was more stuff than I thought."

April noticed a poster dated a decade before. "Many years of stuff."

"Exactly." At the coffee station, Missy poured three mugs. "Fixings right there." She pointed to cups of cream and a tray holding sweeteners.

"Are you keeping all of it?" Shelby added cream to her cup.

"I'm trying to decide," Missy said, running a hand through her red hair. "My predecessor obviously didn't throw anything away, bless her heart."

"Mind if I look around?" Shelby asked.

"Not at all," Missy said.

Shelby began to pace, studying every detail of the room. She peeked inside the closets and the cabinets. She even snapped photos.

April and Missy watched, exchanging smiles.

"She has a real knack for organizing," April said.

"Oh, I know," Missy replied. "I saw her in action at the retreat."

Appearing thoughtful, Shelby approached Missy. "Is it okay if I tell you what I think?"

"Please be my guest," Missy said.

Shelby selected a brochure out of a box. "Now this is obviously outdated, since it says summer of 2008."

The chamber director put a hand to her forehead. "That should have been thrown out years ago."

"But I think you should save one or two of each document," Shelby said. "You need to keep a historic record of what was going on in Magnolia Harbor."

Missy nodded. "Good point. So I'll save two or three copies. I can donate a copy to the historical society for their archives. I'll stack everything else for disposal."

"I can help," Shelby said. "Tell me what to do."

April put her cup of coffee down. "I'll pitch in too."

A couple of hours later, the chamber office was fresh and clean. The closets and cupboards were neatly organized. Missy had called two volunteers to cart away what could be recycled. Other bags went to the nearby trash receptacle.

Missy stood in the middle of the floor and spun in a circle, arms wide. "I feel so free. All that stuff is gone." She gave April and Shelby big hugs. "Thank you so much."

"No problem." Blushing, Shelby said, "Remember those photos I took? With your permission, I'd like to post the before and after pictures on my website. When I get one, that is. If you don't want me to, I'll delete them."

"Shelby is starting an organizing business," April added proudly.

"Of course you can," Missy said. "And I'll also give you a testimonial. We're all about helping small businesses here at the chamber."

"I'm so excited," Shelby said as they drove back to the inn. "My first client."

"And I'm excited for you," April said. "When you make your mind up, you go for it. I admire that." No holding back for Shelby.

No wonder she'd done so well in her career. Which would soon be her former career, April believed.

Shelby handed April her phone. "Can you check the photos for me?" The phone was set to display her picture gallery.

April scrolled through the photos. "These are great." She went back and forth between the before and after shots. "Poor Missy had a ton of old paper."

"Almost literally. Did you see the way that pickup was loaded down?" Shelby was referring to the vehicle the two volunteers had used to take the discarded paper to the recycling center.

A text notification appeared at the top of the phone screen. April hastily averted her eyes but not before she saw the sender. *Devon*. She squirmed in her seat, uncertain whether to say anything or not. It wasn't her business, but Shelby would probably want to know right away.

Shelby glanced over, obviously picking up on her discomfort. "What's the matter?"

April handed the phone back. "You got a text from Devon. It popped up on the screen. I didn't read it."

"I'll read it later." Shelby set her jaw. "Or just delete it."

"It's tough, I know." April's last serious relationship had died slowly. After the first breakup, there had been attempted reconciliations, which soon failed. It had been up to her to finally pull the plug. Sometimes she wondered if she'd done the right thing, especially when she was particularly lonely. But then she remembered a few deal-breaker incidents, and they were enough to steel her heart against regret.

"If you want to talk, I'll be glad to listen," April said. "But no pressure."

They arrived at the inn. Shelby put the car into park and turned off the engine. "I appreciate that. But at the moment I'm going to focus on downloading those photographs." She smiled, but it didn't quite reach her eyes. "And get ready for my date with Trevor."

"You know where to find me," April said lightly, leaving it at that. "I think I'm going to take a long bubble bath and read one of my new books. Did you see the basket of goodies they put in the bathroom?"

"I did. I can't decide between the lavender or honey soap."

"Me either." April grabbed her bag of books.

They arranged to meet in the lobby at six o'clock. They would miss social hour at the inn, but April didn't mind. Shelby was going to drive again unless Dawn and Jamie wanted to go with them to trivia night.

Up in her room, April set her bag down. Suddenly, she wondered what to wear. She went to the closet and flipped through her clothes. Should she wear the pink or the pale-green sweater? April decided on the pink. It flattered her complexion.

Dawn called April's room. "What are you up to?" her friend asked.

April couldn't hold back a giggle. "I have a date tonight."

Dawn's silence was gratifying. "With that good-looking fisherman?" she finally asked. "Or did you meet someone else today?"

"No, it's him. His name is Owen. Shelby and I ran into him and his son at the park." While puttering around the room, April filled Dawn in on the accidental meeting.

"I'm glad to hear Shelby has a date too," Dawn said. "The way that race car driver treated her . . . What a jerk." Shelby had also confided in Dawn and Jamie about her breakup with Devon.

"He might not be totally out of the picture," April said. "He texted her today."

Dawn groaned. "Oh no. I mean, I think oh no. Maybe he regrets dumping her. Maybe they're meant to be together."

April's instincts said no. Devon had fooled around behind Shelby's back, so he wasn't to be trusted. "I'm sure he'll regret it sooner or later.

Shelby's a keeper. She did her first organizing job today. Well, it was pro bono, but she's using the pictures."

"Really? Where was that?" Dawn asked. "She's a go-getter, no question."

April told her about helping Missy organize the chamber of commerce office. "So, Shelby and I are going to miss social hour. We're meeting the guys at the Dragonfly to play some trivia. Do you and Jamie want to come with us?"

Dawn laughed. "I'm not going to be a third wheel. I might scare Owen off."

"Don't be silly," April said. "It's open to everyone."

"I'll talk to Jamie about it," Dawn said. "Maybe we'll see you there."

"Great. I hope so."

"I promise we won't interfere with your dates," Dawn teased before she disconnected.

April picked up one of her new books that Owen had recommended, and it hooked her from the very first page. After reading a few chapters, she dressed in the pink sweater and a nice pair of jeans.

A few minutes before six, April trotted down to the lobby.

Shelby stood in front of the literature rack, rearranging brochures that were in the wrong place. "Why do people do this?" she muttered.

Winston bounded into the room and made a beeline for April.

"Hey, boy." April bent to pat the dog. "How are you tonight?"

He wagged his tail and wiggled with pleasure.

April straightened and turned to Shelby. Her new friend wore a green top that set off her auburn hair, trim tan slacks, and low-heeled boots. "You look nice."

"Thanks. I actually broke out the curling iron." Shelby smiled at April. "So do you. Pink is your color."

"Thank you." April studied Shelby for any sign of distress over

Devon. To April's relief, her friend seemed fine. "Are we ready to roll?" A few butterflies fluttered in her belly at the thought of seeing Owen. She told herself to calm down.

On the way downtown, Shelby said, "I deleted the text. Without reading it." She blinked rapidly.

In the light of an oncoming car, April thought she saw moisture in Shelby's eyes. "Good for you," April said, then decided it was best to change the subject. "I'm excited about tonight. I haven't been on a date in over a year."

"A whole year? Wow." Shelby cringed. "I'm sorry. Was it because you were sick?"

"Yes, and I avoided men like the plague." For a long time, April hadn't even felt human, let alone feminine. She realized she'd come a long way. The fact that she even considered getting close to a member of the opposite sex . . . Now she was jumping the gun again. This was trivia night at a coffee shop, not exactly a romantic outing.

"Well, they definitely aren't avoiding you," Shelby retorted.

They reached downtown, and Shelby slowed, figuring out where to park. A sign indicated a parking lot off Main Street, so she drove there and slid into a spot.

"By the way, we might see Dawn and Jamie here," April said, taking off her seat belt. "I told Dawn about it earlier. She promised they won't interfere with our dates."

"Hopefully, we won't need someone to save us." Shelby chuckled. "Let's pick a code word. If one of us is having a terrible time, we can say it and then we'll leave."

April had to admit it was a good idea. The men could prove to be boors upon closer acquaintance. "What's the code word?"

They discussed it for a minute and finally decided on *stock car race* because it was a phrase they were both unlikely to say. Shelby didn't want to even think about the sport, let alone talk about it, and April had never been a fan of any type of racing.

They got out of the car and strolled down Main Street toward the Dragonfly, where people were already filing in. Most of the other businesses were closed, their windows softly lit to reveal attractive displays.

"There they are." Shelby waved at the two men walking from the other direction.

April waved too, and Owen and Trevor returned the greeting. They met up in front of the coffee shop.

"After you, ladies," Owen said, opening the door.

April and Shelby walked in, followed by Trevor, with Owen bringing up the rear.

The coffee shop was almost full. The only table with four seats was near the podium. April would be sitting front and center on her first date in ages. Oh well, it couldn't be helped.

"How are you tonight?" Owen asked April after they settled into their seats. He rested one arm on the table, his eyes warm and twinkling.

"I'm great," she said. "I spent some time reading one of my new books."

"Me too," Owen responded. "Trevor and I bought out the bookstore."

"We sure did." Trevor picked up a small printed menu featuring the special desserts the coffee shop was offering tonight. "I'm having the peanut butter and chocolate cheesecake."

"That sounds good," April said. When was the last time she'd eaten cheesecake? She was past due for that indulgence.

Angel came over to get their orders. After saying hello and being introduced to Owen and his son, she jotted down their choices. April and Trevor asked for the cheesecake, Shelby went for the cranberry apple crisp, and Owen chose pecan pie with ice cream. They all ordered iced tea.

"Have you been to trivia night before?" Angel asked.

"Not here," Owen said. "At home, yes."

Angel cocked her head, pen poised over her notepad. "And where is that?"

"Charlotte," Trevor said.

Angel glanced at Shelby. "You come from Charlotte too, right?"

"Yes, I do," Shelby said with a smile. "It's nice to connect with someone from home."

Trevor nodded.

"People form teams for trivia," Angel continued. "You could all be one team or two, your choice. Our presenter will display the questions, and you answer them. No phones or tablets allowed. Then we collect the answer sheets and announce the winners."

"How about the four of us on the same team?" Trevor suggested. "You know all kinds of old stuff, Dad. And we know what's going on now."

Owen laughed, a deep, relaxed rumble. "I'm not sure I care for the way you put that."

"You all work it out," Angel said. "You need to decide by the time we pass out the answer sheets." She hurried toward the counter area to prepare their order.

After they all agreed to be on the same team, Trevor said, "Now we need a name."

Angel delivered the desserts and glasses of iced tea, then hurried away again.

April peeled the paper off a straw. "I have no idea what we should be called. I'm terrible at naming things."

"Jamie and Dawn made it," Shelby said, motioning toward the front door.

April turned to wave. They were with Paisley and a man who must be her husband. They pushed two tables together near the back. April wished she had thought of that.

"How about Beauties and the Beasts?" Trevor asked. He folded his arms across his chest, appearing pleased with himself.

Shelby's cheeks flamed. "I can live with that, if you're the Beast," she said to Trevor.

"What did you think I meant?" he said with a teasing grin. "The other way around? No chance."

Owen regarded April with a respectful but admiring gaze. "I think he got it on the first try."

Now April felt heat rush up her neck. "Aren't you a pair of charmers?"

In response, the two men gave her identical cheeky grins.

Despite her mild chiding, April was pleased. It was nice to be considered beautiful, especially by a very attractive man.

Shelby

Shelby caught April's eye and smiled. Her new friend certainly seemed to be having a great time this evening.

"All right, Beauties and the Beasts it is." Shelby had to admit feeling self-conscious but in a good way. *Trevor believes I'm beautiful.* With that thought, a little more of the wound caused by Devon healed.

Angel circled the room with answer sheets. When she arrived at their table, she asked, "Did you make a decision?"

"Yes," Shelby said. "We're one team, the four of us, and our name is Beauties and the Beasts."

"Oh, good choice." Angel grinned. "Who's going to be the recorder?"

"I will," Shelby offered.

Angel passed her the answer sheet. "The wild card gets extra points. Sometimes people snag first place by getting it right. There are prizes for the winners."

Shelby saw twenty-one spaces for answers, the last one labeled a wild card.

"What are the prizes?" April asked.

"We have gift certificates from local businesses." Angel grinned again. "If you win, you might have to share."

"I don't mind sharing," Trevor said to Shelby. "Do you?"

"Of course not," Shelby said. Winning would give them a good excuse to see each other again. But what if they didn't win? She let that thought go and forced herself to focus on the moment. She was nowhere close to dating anyone. Trevor was only a friend, even if he thought she was pretty.

The chatter in the room died down when a brown-haired man in his late thirties approached the podium. "Hi, everyone. Welcome to trivia night. I'm Josh Ford, the owner of this fine establishment."

The audience clapped.

Josh thanked Angel and another server for their hard work and asked the crowd to be generous with tips. "Now let's get started. First I'd like the teams to introduce themselves."

Shelby's heart sank. She disliked introducing herself to groups and having everyone stare at her as she stumbled over her words.

"Please give us the team name and the names of your mates." Josh motioned to Shelby's table. "You go first."

Shelby nudged Trevor. "Want to do the honors?"

Trevor stood. "Hi, everyone. We're Beauties and the Beasts. I'm sure you can guess which is which."

Everyone laughed.

"I'm Trevor, this is my dad, Owen, and these lovely ladies are April and Shelby." He sat down to applause.

The rest of the people around the room named their teams. Dawn and Jamie were on the Old and In the Way team, with Paisley and her husband. Shelby imagined they'd be tough to beat, with a librarian and a teacher on their team.

Josh went through the rules. "No using the Internet, calling home, or whispering answers in the restrooms."

The crowd laughed.

"Okay, question one." Josh pushed a clicker and read the words that appeared on the screen behind his head, "'What is the business term for assets that can be turned into cash immediately?'"

"I know that one. Liquid assets." Shelby wrote the answer down.

Sometimes being an accountant had its advantages.

The rest of the questions were an eclectic mix of pop culture, geography, world history, and science. The wild card question was: Who wrote *The Rose and the Yew Tree* under a pen name? It was a slam dunk for the Beauties and the Beasts, with two mystery buffs at the table. April and Owen both knew that the answer was Agatha Christie.

Shelby's phone chimed, and more out of curiosity than anything, she glanced at it. *Devon.* Again? Guilt curled behind her breastbone. What if something was wrong? It wasn't like him to keep contacting her if she didn't answer. "Excuse me," she said to her companions. "I'll be right back."

She hurried to the restroom and ducked into a stall for privacy. With trembling fingers, she opened the message. *Shelby, I don't blame you for not answering. But I meant it.*

Meant what? Shelby gritted her teeth in frustration. She'd erased his message without reading it. She searched her phone to see if the text was still there. *Nope. Gone.*

She held the phone in her palm, now slick with perspiration. She didn't want anything to do with Devon, right? She should delete this message too and pretend she never saw it. Better yet, block him. Let his missives go into the void.

But what if?

The restroom door swung open, and light footsteps approached. "Shelby? It's April. Are you okay?"

Shelby swallowed, then said, "How did you know something was wrong?"

April moved closer to the stall door. "I could tell by the expression on your face when you left the table." She paused. "Is it Devon?"

"Yes," Shelby admitted. She opened the door and stepped out.

"He texted me again." She showed April the phone. "But I have no idea what he said the first time because I deleted it."

"And now you're curious," April said as she handed the phone back. "I would be too."

"You think I should reply?" Shelby felt as if poised on the brink of a precipice. Should she jump and hope she landed safely? Or stay where she was and always wonder?

"I can't answer that for you," April said. "But if the idea of talking to him disturbs you, then listen to your gut."

Was she disturbed? Or excited and relieved? She couldn't decide. But for once, she did the wise thing. She turned off her phone. "I'm going to wait and see how I feel in the morning."

April patted her shoulder. "Good idea. Now let's go see who won the game."

Josh was getting ready to announce the winners as Shelby and April returned to the table. "It was close tonight," he said. "Only one point apart for our two top teams. The winners are . . ." He paused, increasing the tension in the room. "Beauties and the Beasts!"

The room erupted into applause, and the teammates exchanged excited glances.

Josh waved at them. "Come on up." He gave each member a gift certificate to The Tidewater. "Congratulations."

Shelby tucked her gift certificate into her purse as they went back to their seats.

"Who's up for a walk around downtown?" Trevor asked the table at large.

"I'm going to drive April to the inn," Owen said.

"I'll go with you, Trevor," Shelby said. "I can drop you off later." She was glad he didn't want the evening to end yet. Neither did she.

The group parted ways outside the coffee shop.

Shelby and Trevor strolled along the quiet streets, lights from house windows streaming onto the sidewalk. The cold air had moderated due to a warm front moving in, along with cloud cover.

"This is such a pretty little town," Shelby remarked.

"Agreed." Trevor walked close but not too close. "It feels like stepping back in time."

They talked about their mutual hometown of Charlotte, how the city had grown, bringing new riches and opportunities along with the influx of people and businesses. Shelby danced around the topic of racing, which was a main economic driver.

Thankfully, Trevor wasn't a racing fan. "I prefer fishing. Sitting in a hot stadium listening to engines roar isn't my idea of fun."

"My dad likes to go fishing," Shelby said. "Whenever he gets time off. Which isn't often." She explained that he had his own business.

They wandered down to the lake and stood on the upper dock, gazing into the inky water.

"I know what that's like," Trevor said, leaning both elbows on the railing. "This is about the only downtime we're going to have for a while. Once the weather moderates, they'll be pouring slabs for the new houses."

"Any of your clients need an organizer?" Shelby laughed at her boldness. But the people Trevor built homes for sounded ideal for her services—wealthy enough to pay for an organizer with houses large enough to need one.

"I'll bet they do," Trevor said. "Some of them have housekeepers. They're usually dual-career families. They build big beautiful houses, but they're never home to enjoy them."

"What a waste." Shelby was driven, but she hoped to keep some balance in her life. "With my new business, I'm going to work from home." Every time she said something about her goal, it became more real.

"Our office is at Dad's house," Trevor said. "He's been doing the books himself, but I've been telling him to hire someone."

Shelby's pulse jumped. "A bookkeeper?"

"Yeah," Trevor said. In the light of the dock light, he flashed a grin. "Know anyone?"

"I might," Shelby said, her mind beginning to whir. If she could line up one or two steady bookkeeping gigs, then maybe she could make the leap. "I've been thinking I could do accounting on the side as I build up the organizing business."

"Sounds like a good plan," he said. "Tell me more about your organizing business."

"Well, it's still in development," Shelby admitted. "But I had my first job today. Right after we saw you and your dad in the park."

"Seriously? What happened?"

"It was at the chamber of commerce." Shelby explained how she and April had volunteered to help Missy, then moved on to her ideas for other types of organizing jobs.

Trevor was a great listener, taking it all in and asking intelligent questions.

"It's wonderful talking to you," she said. "You understand all the ins and outs of starting a business."

He rubbed his chin with his thumb and forefinger. "Well, I watched Dad do it. I was a young teenager when he went out on his own."

"You have two older brothers, right?" Shelby remembered him mentioning them. "Are they involved?"

Trevor nodded. "Blake is a plumber, and Jack is an electrician. We use them all the time. It works out well." At her further questioning, he told her that both of his brothers were married and had kids. "I have a lot of fun being Uncle Trev."

Shelby smiled. She was a "lonely only," as she called herself. But some of her friends were getting married now, and a couple of them had babies. She enjoyed babysitting sometimes and looked forward to having her own family someday.

The wind began to gust, and by mutual unspoken consent, they walked off the dock, heading back to Shelby's car. The first few drops of rain started falling by the time they reached the parking lot.

"We made it just in time," Shelby said, unlocking the car.

Trevor turned his face up to the sky. "At least it's not snow."

Sitting inside the car with Trevor was cozy, made even more so by the swish of the wipers. The Tidewater wasn't far from downtown, and Shelby drove slowly to stretch out the drive. She didn't want to say good night yet.

Being with Trevor was comforting and safe, like snuggling up in a blanket in front of a fire. Even better, she liked who she was with Trevor. Not once had she wondered if she was interesting enough, if she was saying the right thing, or if she was holding his attention. Those were all the things she'd wondered whenever she was with Devon.

Maybe she'd never see Trevor again after she left Magnolia Harbor. But she wouldn't forget how he made her feel.

As if she were standing on solid ground.

17

Grace

Grace closed the door to her quarters with a sigh of relief. It had been a long day, and she couldn't wait to finally relax with her library book.

Winston hopped into his favorite chair and curled up, his sigh expressing everything she felt.

Although Grace had told her sister and aunt that she planned to read a book with Winston in the afternoon, she'd ended up working around the inn instead. After the morning session, Grace had freshened the guest linens, cleaned the public rooms, and taken care of paperwork. Running the inn meant always looking ahead. As soon as the retreat was over, new guests were coming in, and she had reservations to process and e-mails to write.

Grace took a shower and changed into comfortable yoga pants and a fleece top. Then she sat on the sofa and checked her phone.

There was a text from Spencer. *Hoping to be fully recovered by tomorrow morning. Remind me to do something extra nice for you in the future.*

She wrote back, glad he was almost over the flu, and soon they were exchanging a volley of texts. Grace smiled at the wit and sense of humor he displayed despite still being under the weather. He really was a wonderful man.

She set the phone aside and patted the cushion. "Come sit with me, Winston. You're my other favorite guy in Magnolia Harbor." She had to specify the city, because her son, Jake, had to be on her list of favorite guys, and he lived in Raleigh, North Carolina.

Thinking of Jake, she picked up the phone again and sent a note. He was only in his twenties, so of course he was very busy.

Jake wrote right back, promising a call soon to catch up.

Her maternal duty done, Grace picked up her book and opened it. Reading was the perfect way to unwind, and soon Grace nodded off.

A rapping sound woke her with a start. Her sudden movement sent the book sliding toward the floor. Grace caught it and sat up. Someone was knocking on her door.

Winston, instead of barking, leaped off the sofa and went to the door, whining. That meant it was someone he liked.

Grace opened the door to find Maya standing there, arms wrapped around her midsection. Her heart gave a leap of concern at seeing that Maya's hair was disheveled and there were deep shadows under her eyes. "Come in."

"I'm sorry to bother you," Maya said, remaining in the doorway. She ran a hand through her hair. "But . . ." Her bottom lip trembled, and she blinked rapidly.

"You're not bothering me," Grace said. She gently ushered her into the room. "Please have a seat. I was just sitting here, reading a book." She didn't mention that she'd been napping.

Maya perched on an armchair.

Winston leaped up into her lap, and Maya squeaked.

"You surprised me," Maya said with a little laugh. She began petting him. "This sweet fellow spent some time with me this morning."

"He likes to visit," Grace said, sitting on the sofa. She glanced around. She didn't have anything to offer Maya except a glass of water.

Someone else knocked on the door, and a second later, Charlotte poked her head inside the room. "Oh, I didn't know you had company. I came to see if you wanted a cup of chai tea before bed."

Grace glanced at Maya. "How does chai tea sound?"

Maya was still focused on petting the appreciative Winston. "I'd love a cup." She gave Charlotte a watery smile. "And an oatmeal cookie, if you have some left."

Charlotte tapped the doorjamb. "There sure are. I'll be right back."

"How did the session go this morning?" Maya asked. "I'm really sorry about dumping it on you."

Grace shrugged. To be honest, she had been worried at first, but there had been no harm done. "It went fine. We've got a great group of ladies."

"We do." Maya sighed, a deep exhale that seemed to hold a world of sorrow.

Charlotte returned with a tray. "Here we go." She set the tray on the coffee table and passed around mugs, then a plate of cookies. She sat down on the sofa beside Grace. "Quiet evening. I think our guests are still out."

"They went to trivia night at the Dragonfly," Grace said.

"Oh yeah," her sister said. "Dean told me about that. But it's hard for him to get time off in the evening." She smiled. "That's one thing I don't miss about restaurant life."

"I love this tea," Grace said after a moment. The brew was rich and creamy, with hints of cinnamon. It tasted delicious with an oatmeal cookie.

"Me too," Charlotte said. "It makes a nice change from coffee and regular tea. And it doesn't keep me awake, because this particular batch is decaf."

While they chatted, Maya sat quietly, staring into her mug.

During a lull in the conversation, Maya squared her shoulders, seeming to come to a resolve. "I'm glad you joined us, Charlotte. I find myself in a most difficult predicament." She grabbed a tissue from a nearby box and dabbed at her eyes. "I'm not sure I can finish the retreat."

Charlotte exchanged an alarmed glance with Grace. "What's wrong, Maya? Are you ill?"

"No, but I feel like a fake." Maya gulped back a sob. "My whole life is falling apart, and here I am, telling other people what to do."

"First of all, you have our unqualified support," Grace assured their guest. "Don't worry about the retreat right now." If being an innkeeper for several years had taught her anything, it was that they would handle it somehow. "We're more worried about you."

"You are too kind," Maya said. "Really wonderful, in fact." She sniffled a bit more, then said quietly, "My husband left me."

"I'm so sorry," Grace said. She had friends who had gone through divorce and had witnessed the devastating impact it could wreak. No matter who left or who was at fault, a marriage breakdown tore a home apart, plain and simple.

Maya nodded in acknowledgment. "We've been having issues for a while. And we had a terrible fight before I left to come here." Her face twisted in anguish. "He told me he won't be home when I get back."

Grace could only imagine how difficult it was to go through such painful turmoil while hundreds of miles away from home. "If you want to leave, we'll figure it out on this end." Maybe she could take over the rest of the retreat. It wouldn't be the same, but she didn't want the ladies to lose momentum. They could also give partial refunds.

To her surprise, Maya shook her head. "He's not there right now. He had a trip planned to the West Coast. So my main concern is the retreat. This situation has made it very clear that I'm not practicing what I preach." She gave a bitter laugh. "It's obvious that I don't have it all together."

Charlotte made a gentle snort. "Who does? We can only do our best, and sometimes life happens in spite of it."

Grace could attest to that. She'd done her best to create a

happy home for her husband and young son. But then Hank had died suddenly and tragically. An idea blossomed in her mind. "I'm going to make a suggestion," she said. "But I'll understand if you don't like it, okay?"

"Please do," Maya said. "I'm fresh out of ideas." She put her hand close to her face. "All I can see is my problem."

Grace took another moment to organize her thoughts. "Maya, you have a true gift. We've seen it firsthand this week. The women attending the retreat are fired up and excited about life. They had deep desires they struggled to put into action. Until you came into their lives."

Maya laughed. "What a tribute. Thanks for saying that."

"It's true," Charlotte added. "I'm even more excited about what we're doing here at the inn. For me, the retreat has confirmed that I'm on the right track."

"Me too," Grace said. "And I sure am relieved."

Everyone laughed.

Grace hesitated, then plunged ahead. "But let me ask you this. Is doing this kind of teaching still your North Star?" She held her breath, waiting for Maya's answer.

A few moments went by, and then Maya nodded. "Encouraging other people to use their gifts and follow their dreams is what I was born to do. Even in the face of adversity." Her expression was wistful as she gently set Winston aside and stood. "I think I need to dig deep and refocus on my work."

"That's fantastic news," Grace said. "Please let us know if we can do anything to help."

"Thank you." Maya walked to the door. "I'll be ready to teach tomorrow morning. You can count on it."

After the door shut behind Maya, Grace collapsed back into the sofa cushions. "Whew. I am so glad she's not leaving. Crisis averted."

"I really hope everything works out with her marriage. She's a wonderful woman." Charlotte picked up a cookie and took a bite.

"She is indeed," Grace said.

Winston cocked his head and regarded her with bright eyes, then did a little dance.

"Want to go out?" Grace had already locked the doggy door, so she would have to let him outside. "I'll take the tray to the kitchen, if you want."

"Thanks," Charlotte said, sounding thoughtful. She grabbed another cookie. "I guess I'll wander over to the cottage." She kissed her sister on the cheek. "Good night."

Grace gave her a hug. "Sleep well. And see you in the morning." She loaded the tray with the empty mugs and picked it up. "All right, Winston, let's go."

Maya was the first one downstairs the next morning. She seemed rested and calm. "Good morning," she said at the kitchen doorway.

"Help yourself to coffee," Grace said. She was cutting up a fresh pineapple that oozed juice and sweet aroma. "Breakfast will be ready soon."

"We're having scrambled eggs and popovers with bacon," Charlotte said. She opened the oven and pulled out a pan of lofty delights. "Perfect, if I do say so myself."

"They're gorgeous," Maya said, pouring a cup of coffee. "I'm pleased to report that I have an appetite today. Not having one while staying here is a shame."

Grace smiled at the instructor. "I'm glad. We're thinking of adding a tagline 'Pack a hearty appetite when you stay at the Magnolia Harbor Inn.'"

Charlotte whirled around, regarding her sister with wide eyes. "Seriously?"

"No," Grace said. "But it's true, isn't it?"

"I hope people enjoy the food." Charlotte winked. "It's what I live for. Well, that and other things."

At Grace's invitation, Maya settled at the island to sip her coffee. Winston begged until Grace put him on the stool beside her, so he could be near his new buddy.

"I'm a little nervous," Maya confessed, reaching out to rub Winston's ears. "I don't often talk about myself when I teach. I keep the focus on my students."

"It's going to be fine," Grace said. "The students are all very kind and accepting people." She even felt comfortable saying that about the out-of-town guests, who were definitely lovely women.

Maya smiled. "If someone is going to go through a crisis, then the Magnolia Harbor Inn is the spot to do it. I've never been in such a warm, welcoming place."

Charlotte glanced at Grace. "Another new tagline? 'Come see us when you're having a crisis.'"

Grace laughed. "I don't think so. Although I do admit that the inn has a healing touch."

April

For the first time in months, April woke up without a dark cloud hanging over her head. She stayed in bed for a moment, stretching. She searched for aches and pains, twinges and soreness, but she felt fine from head to toe. She was finally and truly on the mend.

A huge grin broke across her face. *Thank You.*

As she threw back the covers, she thought about the previous evening. After leaving the coffee shop, Owen had dropped her off at the inn. But first they had taken a drive along a route that provided a view of the little town below, lights twinkling in the darkness.

The conversation had stayed on light topics, although Owen briefly mentioned the loss of his wife. She had died about five years ago.

The memory made April pause on her way to the shower, her good spirits suddenly plummeting with trepidation. She hadn't told Owen about her battle with cancer.

And now in the clear light of day, April realized why. She hadn't wanted to scare him off. He'd already lost his wife, and he was unlikely to want to get involved with a woman diagnosed with cancer. Not that she thought anything permanent was going to come of their budding friendship. For one thing, they lived more than a hundred miles apart, according to the online map she'd checked.

April shook her head at her own foolishness and cautioned herself to take it one step at a time. She didn't need to burden Owen with the story of her illness. If she even saw him again.

Her phone, which was resting on the nightstand, lit up and vibrated.

She turned around and saw a message from Owen. *Had a great time last night. Trevor and I are headed to the beach to do some surf casting. Have a wonderful day.*

It wasn't exactly another date, but he was checking in with her. That was promising.

April wrote back that she'd also had a great time and extended her well-wishes for a safe trip.

Magnolia Harbor wasn't very far from the ocean. She had checked the map earlier and found that they were about an hour away from Charleston. If they weren't so busy with the retreat—and it wasn't January—she might head over to the beach too. Since she lived in the mountains, dipping her toes into ocean water was a rare event.

April hurried through dressing for the day, eager to get downstairs for breakfast. She was starving. Something about this place had improved her appetite. Of course, it also helped that food finally tasted good again.

Hello, taste buds. You decided to wake up in the right place. April laughed as she charged down the stairs.

When April entered the dining room, she saw that the other women were already gathered. Some were lined up at the buffet, and others were eating at the table. A gentle buzz of chatter and laughter filled the room.

Jamie waved to April. "Popovers," she said, holding one up.

April joined Jamie at the buffet table. "I love popovers." She took one, then gave herself healthy servings of scrambled eggs and bacon and a spoonful of fruit salad. As she took a seat next to Dawn, she glanced around. "Where's Shelby?"

"She hasn't come down yet," Dawn said.

April hoped Shelby was all right. She wondered if her friend was upset about Devon.

"Did you two have a good time last night?" Dawn asked, elbowing April.

"Yes, spill the beans," Jamie said to April. "Not only did your team win first prize, but you were with the best-looking men in the place."

"We had a great time," April said. "After we left the coffee shop, Owen and I ended up taking a drive before he brought me back here." She shrugged. "We're still getting to know each other."

Dawn nodded. "Take your time. You're just getting your feet wet in the dating pool again."

"Thanks for reminding me." April felt slightly relieved by Dawn's comment. She told herself that she didn't need to put a lot of weight on her time with Owen. In the past, it seemed that everything happened so fast. She would be in a relationship after only a few dates. She wasn't going to do that again.

Shelby entered the dining room, walking with her head down.

"Uh-oh," Dawn said. "I wonder what's going on with Shelby."

There was an empty chair beside Jamie, and she patted it when Shelby came over with her breakfast. "Have a seat."

"Good morning, everyone," Shelby said as she sat down. Then she busied herself with lining up her silverware, settling her napkin, and taking the first few bites.

April decided to let Shelby be until a more private moment. And maybe she was groggy still, not quite awake. "The retreat is flying by," April remarked. "But I feel like I've packed months into only a few days."

"Me too," Dawn said. "I wrote a chapter yesterday."

"That's great," April said.

"Of course it will probably change a lot," Dawn said. "But at least I got the words down."

"How about you, Jamie?" April said. "Did you make progress on your sketch?"

Jamie nodded. "I finished it, and now I'm ready to start painting."

"Wonderful," Dawn said. "I can't wait to see it."

Maya, at the other end of the table, stood up. "Good morning, ladies. How are you doing today?"

As the attendees chorused greetings and updates, their leader smiled and nodded.

April noticed that Maya had a lightness around her eyes, a release of tension. April was glad to see that the woman was feeling better.

"We're going to convene the class soon," Maya said. "This is the time to get coffee refills or take a restroom break. Let's meet in the living room in ten minutes." She inhaled deeply.

April realized that Maya was nervous. That was interesting. Until now, Maya had worn poised confidence like a shield. April drained her cup. "I'm going to get a refill." After clearing her plate, she filled her mug and grabbed a bottle of water.

The others did the same, and then they took their usual seats in the living room.

April thought it was interesting how people found a spot and kept returning to it. She saw it all the time at school. Sometimes she made the children change seats temporarily so they could talk to different classmates.

Maya watched as everyone got settled. Once the ladies were quiet, she said, "I'm going to do something a little different today. It's not on the agenda."

Perhaps sensing Maya's serious mood, no one called out comments or made any jokes. If anything, the students became even more attentive as they waited.

Their instructor paced back and forth, her expression serious. "This is new for me, so please forgive me if my presentation is less than polished. Let me take a step back. My whole business of teaching is about helping people, mostly women, live their best lives. I try to help them figure out where they're stuck, identify their gifts, and set a new course when the old one isn't working." Her voice lowered to a whisper. "And I'm supposed to be an example of that. But I'm not. At least, not at the moment."

A hush fell over the room, and April had the sense they were all holding their breath. She certainly was. Her heart ached for the instructor.

Maya bowed her head for a moment, then looked up. "My husband, Max, and I are a two-career couple. My work takes me all over the country. He's a cardiologist and very busy, and he's often away from home too. When we got married, we were desperately in love. But now, ten years later, we've grown apart." She put a hand on a nearby chair, as if for support. "Max told me our marriage is over."

A tide of groans and exclamations of dismay filled the room.

Maya straightened, curling both hands into fists. "I hope we can work it out. I'm certainly going to try. But until then . . ." Her voice trailed off.

"You hang on, have faith, and pray," Winnie said stoutly. "And we're behind you, aren't we, girls?"

Winnie's words were joined by other women who expressed support and care.

Maya sank into an armchair and bent forward, hands over her face. "Sorry. I'm overwhelmed. You're all so wonderful."

"So are you," Jamie said. "Because of you, I'm doing art again. I sketched out a painting."

"Really?" Maya asked. "Already? Today's assignment was to take the first baby steps toward your goal."

"We're already there," April said. "I went on a date last night."

"And I wrote a chapter," Dawn said.

"I had my first client," Shelby added. "It was pro bono, but I got pictures and a testimonial."

Maya's brows rose higher with each remark. "I'm so proud of you all. You sure are fast learners."

"No, you're a great teacher," Jamie said. She snapped her fingers. "It was like a light bulb went off. I was waiting for someone to give me permission to return to my art. I gave it to myself."

Grace put up a hand. "Remember that movie where the teacher's opus was the students he taught? Well, we're your opus, Maya."

"I never thought of it that way," Maya said. "Thank you." After a moment, she stood and clapped. "All right, class." Her smile was teasing as she called them that, like a strict old-school teacher. "Let's go around and talk about baby steps."

April shared a little about her night out and her plans to be open to more dates, then listened as the other women spoke.

Maya gently coached each woman in breaking down her goal and identifying first steps. "Many people have the tendency to set a big goal, and they eventually quit when it seems overwhelming. New Year's resolutions are the perfect example. How many people resolve to lose weight or start exercising? If they started small, like a ten-minute walk each day, then they might not give up by February."

April could relate. She'd abandoned many resolutions in the past. She considered her current goal. If she approached men with marriage in mind, she would be putting the cart way before the horse. She needed to slow down and get to know her dates.

They were taking a break when April noticed Shelby hurrying from the room. Something about the younger woman's hunched shoulders and expression worried her. Realizing she might be intruding, she went after her anyway. Shelby was already halfway to the stairs when April caught up with her. "Is everything okay?"

Shelby shook her head. "I'm so confused. I'm afraid I've made the biggest mistake of my life."

Shelby

April put her arm around Shelby. "Do you want to talk about it?"

Shelby nodded. Her tendency was to figure out things on her own, a legacy of being an only child, she supposed. Having friends to bounce situations off of was a relief. And in this case, she certainly couldn't discuss it with her mother.

"Let go into the music room," April suggested. She ushered Shelby into the room and flipped on the light switch.

They sat in adjacent chairs near the hearth.

"I made a mistake," Shelby said. "And now it's opened up a big can of worms."

"What's that?" April asked, her voice gentle. "Is it about Devon?"

"Yes. I didn't delete his second text. Or the one after that." Shelby took her phone out of her pocket and located Devon's message. *I don't blame you for ignoring me. I'm a jerk, okay? A jerk who messed up the best part of his life. Where are you? Your mom wouldn't tell me.*

"Did you respond to him?" April asked.

"I should have ignored him, but I told him it was over," Shelby answered, setting the phone aside. "He didn't listen, and now my in-box is blowing up. He wants to get back together."

"No more racetrack model?" April asked wryly.

"According to him, after I walked off, he realized what an idiot he was." Shelby frowned, a ball of confusion rolling in her belly. "I don't know whether or not to believe him."

"Take my word on this," April said. "A really solid guy won't cheat."

Tears burned in her eyes. "Devon said he's a fool. All the attention he's been getting lately went to his head." He hadn't put it exactly like that, but Shelby guessed what he meant.

"I'm sure that's true," April said. "Not that I know any celebrities personally, but it's a common enough story." She hesitated. "Is that the life you want for yourself? A famous husband?"

Shelby laughed. "Husband? I wasn't thinking that far ahead." *That's not true.* "Actually, I was imagining it. I had daydreams about us getting married, buying a big house, and living like Charlotte royalty."

Hearing that admission took the air out of her lungs. "I can't believe I said that." Shelby shook her head. "I see it all the time through my job, of course, the glamorous lives of the winning racers. Their gorgeous wives and cute little families. When the most attractive up-and-coming racer asked me out, how could I say no?"

"I get it," April said. "You were living the dream, as they say. But is it *your* dream? There are no right or wrong answers. Only you can decide."

Shelby pictured Devon, his boyish yet devastating charm, his athletic grace and sharp wit. His incredible focus that had made her feel pretty special. Until he focused on someone else. If he'd cheated on her once, then he'd do it again. She was sure of it.

Shelby picked up the phone. "All right, I'm doing it."

"Doing what?" April asked.

"I'm telling him to stop contacting me." Shelby texted Devon saying exactly that. Then she did the next logical thing. "And I'm blocking him." That way he couldn't argue with her decision or try to get around it. The tension drained out of her body. For better or worse, it was done.

"Ready to go back to the session?" April asked.

In a decisive move, Shelby turned off her phone. It was time for her to concentrate on the retreat and her new business, not her love life.

At lunch, Maya made an announcement. "Tomorrow will be really busy. In addition to aromatherapy and massage, Nina Briscoe from Charleston is coming in to do your makeovers."

The women gasped as they exchanged excited glances. Nina was a nationally known style consultant.

"Nina Briscoe?" Missy said, sounding impressed. "I've read about her in several lifestyle magazines."

"Yes, she's wonderful." Maya patted her stylish hair. "She showed me how to change my look when I started to book retreats. I wasn't sure how to dress after being in corporate America for so long."

Shelby considered her wardrobe, which was divided between casual and work. Her work clothes consisted of dress slacks and blouses. She definitely needed a new wardrobe for her business. Something more relaxed but not messy, of course. A professional organizer should appear neat but fashionable, like the women she would be helping. The wives of the race car drivers, maybe. She might as well use those contacts.

"I'm sure you'll all enjoy your sessions with Nina," Maya said. "And this afternoon you'll have personal time. You can work on your one-year action steps or simply relax."

Jamie raised her hand. "Do we have to stay on-site?"

"No, there's no requirement to remain at the inn," Maya said. "Take a walk, go to town, whatever you want. I personally find a change of scene to be beneficial to my creativity and well-being."

"What are you thinking, Jamie?" Dawn asked.

Jamie leaned close, whispering behind her hand. "Road trip to the beach. It's only about an hour from here. We can buzz down there and back and still make dinner."

"The water is too cold to go swimming," Dawn reminded her.

"So what?" Jamie said. "We can walk on the beach and enjoy the sunshine and the breeze in our hair. It's a shame to be this close to the coast and not visit the ocean."

"She's right," April said. "Owen is surf casting today. After he told me that, I was thinking how much I would love to go to the beach."

"Where did he go?" Dawn asked.

"I don't know, but I could ask him," April said. Her fair skin flamed pink.

Shelby realized that seeing Owen most likely meant running into Trevor. How did she feel about that? Maybe it would be a good test. She had enjoyed his company last night, and she could see how she felt about him today.

"Go ahead and ask him," Dawn said. "We can use a recommendation where to go."

April pulled out her phone and sent a text. A moment later, she said, "He's at Folly Beach near the lighthouse. He says it's a great wildlife area. Plus, there are shops in town. But a lot of them are closed this time of year."

Jamie jumped up. "Pack your bags, ladies. We're going to the beach."

Fifteen minutes later, they met in the lobby with their totes containing sunglasses, sunscreen, painting supplies, and notebooks. Charlotte gave them a container of homemade cookies and several bottles of water. Then the foursome hopped into Dawn's car and headed out of town.

Shelby sat in the back seat with April, watching the passing countryside and writing notes for her business plan. She'd found an outline on the Internet and was using that as a guide.

She considered one of the questions: Who were her target customers? People without the time, skill, or interest in organizing.

And who were willing to pay. Shelby had found hourly rates ranging from thirty dollars an hour to more than a hundred. As an accountant, she knew that taxes would take a big bite, so thirty would not cut it. Besides, she wouldn't be organizing forty hours a week.

A doubt trickled in. Would she be able to make enough money to pay her bills?

"Deep in thought?" April asked with a smile. She passed Shelby a bottle of water.

"Kind of. I'm working on my business plan." Shelby uncapped the water and took a sip. "Trying to decide how much to charge people per hour."

"You could charge by the project instead," April suggested. "I mean, you'll need to figure out how long it will take. But people might like that better than open-ended hours."

They discussed Shelby's fledgling business most of the way.

"I really appreciate your input," Shelby said. "I'm going to spend a lot of time planning before I take the plunge." She was eager to get her business going, but her innate prudence warned her to slow down.

"Why not do a few clients on the weekends to start with?" April asked. "You don't even have to quit your job or make a formal announcement."

"That's a great idea," Shelby said. She would be able to learn as she went along and make adjustments without jeopardizing her livelihood.

Dawn parked alongside the road. "We'll walk to the beach from here." She retrieved a couple of blankets from the trunk.

The women gathered their totes and started out.

Shelby took deep breaths of the ocean breeze, enjoying the smell of salt and sand. The sound of breakers on the beach was audible, a regular pause and rumble. Overhead, gulls circled.

They met people coming from the other direction and exchanged smiles and nods. Everyone seemed happy to be here on this bright afternoon.

When they reached the end of the road, they took a trail through the dunes to the beach. The view of sky and water opened up. Two men stood near the edge of the water, casting lines into the waves.

Trevor and his dad. Shelby stopped to watch for a moment, caught by their graceful movements, and then she followed the others to a spot in the sand.

"How's this?" Dawn asked, spreading out one of the blankets.

"Perfect," April said. "I'm going to say hello to Owen. Want to come, Shelby?"

Jamie made shooing motions. "Go ahead. We'll be right here."

Shelby and April trudged through the white sand to the packed wet area left by the receding tide. Seagulls followed. A few people were sitting in chairs or strolling along the edge of the water.

"This is wonderful," Shelby said. "I'm so glad we did this."

"Me too. I always forget how much I love the ocean." April stretched her arms wide, face lifted toward the sky.

The two men turned to watch them approach.

Shelby waved and smiled, then joined Trevor. "How's it going?"

"We caught a few fish but released them." Trevor reached into the pocket of his vest. "I found this for you." He handed her a ribbed white shell about five inches long.

"What is it?" Shelby asked. "It's beautiful."

"It's called an angel wing," he said. "The scientific name isn't as pretty."

Shelby smiled at him. "I love it. Thank you."

"I always think it means good things are coming." Trevor shrugged. "I know that probably sounds foolish."

"No, it doesn't." Shelby studied the finely detailed shell, a natural work of art. "I think you're right. Good things *are* coming."

20

Grace

After lunch, Grace, Charlotte, and Winnie helped Maya prepare for the next day's makeovers. They rearranged the music room for private consultations with Nina. Massages and aromatherapy sessions were to be held in Grace's quarters and at Charlotte's cottage.

"Everyone is going to feel so pampered," Charlotte said as they admired the music room. An antique screen had been set up for a changing space and a mirror and a stool moved in for makeup lessons. "I can't wait."

"Me either," Grace said, shifting a vase of flowers to a better spot. Then she put her hand to her mouth with a gasp. "I still need to buy an outfit. I've been so busy this week that I completely forgot."

Maya had suggested that each woman bring or purchase a favorite outfit for the group photo on the last day of the retreat. Grace had tagged the idea as an excuse to buy something new, since she hadn't bought clothes in ages.

"We can go to town this afternoon," Charlotte suggested.

"Good idea," Grace said. She turned to Maya. "Would you like to join us?"

Maya shook her head. "Thanks for the invitation, but I'm going to stay here. I'm composing a letter to Max."

Grace patted Maya's shoulder. "That's important. Good luck with it."

"Thanks. I've already ripped up two versions." Maya smiled. "But I'm getting there."

Charlotte drove them to town in her car, the radio tuned to an oldies station. Now and then she joined in. "I'm practicing for the choir," she said.

Grace studied her sister's pretty face, smiling as she achieved a few high notes. Both Grace and Charlotte were members of the church choir. Charlotte had a beautiful singing voice and was a frequent soloist.

"We hardly ever go anywhere together just for fun," Grace remarked. Yes, they worked side by side and spent many hours in each other's company. But they were usually doing tasks related to the inn.

"You're right." Charlotte turned down the radio slightly. "We should do it more often."

"We'll need to pencil it into the schedule," Grace said. "Otherwise, we get too busy." If there wasn't something going on at the inn, Charlotte was now spending time with Dean. Grace completely supported that, of course. She thought they made a wonderful couple.

"How are things with Dean?" she asked.

Charlotte grinned. "Great. It's nice dating someone who shares my obsession with food."

"Our taste buds thank you," Grace said. "Speaking of which, what are we doing for dinner tonight?" They had decided to serve something for their in-house guests.

"I was thinking everyone could make their own pizzas," Charlotte said. "I already have the dough and toppings ready. It'll be simple and tasty."

"Good choice," Grace said. She pointed. "There's a parking space." For a weekday, downtown sure was busy.

After they got out and were walking up the sidewalk toward Main Street, Charlotte asked, "How's Spencer doing?"

"He's feeling even better and said he's going to try to get out this afternoon," Grace said. "He's been cooped up for days."

Charlotte shuddered. "He had a nasty bug. I'm glad we haven't gotten it." She was silent for a moment. "Do you ever think that you'll start dating him? Officially, I mean." Her grin was wicked.

"Charlotte!" Grace gave her sister a mock tap on the shoulder. "We're just friends. And I like it that way."

"Yeah, I get it. For a long time, I felt that way about Dean too." Charlotte shrugged. "I think I was afraid to change things. I didn't want to mess up our friendship." She paused to examine a window display featuring antique kitchen items.

"Spencer and I have a great time together." Grace reflected on how much she had come to depend upon his friendship. He was there whenever she needed him, whether for an inn emergency, a companion at an event, or someone to talk to. "Friends are rare and valuable commodities."

"We're luckier than most," Charlotte said. "I love our Magnolia Harbor friends. I think this retreat has even deepened our friendships." She reached for the store door. "Mind if we go in for a second?"

"Of course not." Grace followed her sister into the antique shop, which had a familiar aroma of old wood, paper, and dust. She'd spent a lot of time in antique stores and at auctions buying furniture and other household items for the inn.

As Charlotte browsed through antique kitchen utensils, which she collected for photo shoots, Grace continued their conversation. "Talking about people's dreams really forges relationships. I feel quite close to our guests after sitting in a couple of sessions with them."

"Those women are very special," Charlotte said. She held up a gadget. "Can you guess what this is?"

"No, I have no idea," Grace said.

"It's an ice shaver," Charlotte said. "You put ice in the cup, and the handle pushes it through the disk." She turned it over to check the price. "I'm going to buy it. We can make our own snow cones."

"You always liked those." Grace remembered visiting a little market with her sister, who would beg for a snow cone, preferably blue raspberry. Charlotte's lips would be stained the rest of the day.

"I still do," Charlotte said brightly. She paid for the item, and they continued down the street to Miss Millie's dress shop.

Sophie Mah greeted them warmly when they walked in. "How are you both doing?"

They knew Sophie as customers and through the chamber of commerce.

"We're great," Grace answered. "How about you?"

"Very well, thank you. I've had a good week, thanks to you two, I think." Sophie smiled. "Some ladies staying at the inn stopped by."

"Oh yes, they were raving about your store. Now it's our turn to shop." Charlotte began leafing through a rack of dresses. "We're both looking for something a little dressy for dinner parties and special occasions."

Sophie immediately went into action and found Grace and Charlotte several outfits. Soon the sisters were trying on clothing in adjacent changing rooms.

Grace slipped into a blue silk dress with an embossed floral design. The bodice was fitted while the skirt flared around her knees. It was very feminine, and she liked the rustling sound the skirt made when she moved.

"What do you think?" Charlotte asked outside the curtain.

Grace stepped out to see Charlotte in a rayon paisley print dress in rust and cream, with a ruffled hem and wrap bodice. "I like it," Grace said. "The color goes great with your hair and eyes." Charlotte had the unusual combination of brown eyes and blonde hair.

"I want to wear it with my brown boots," Charlotte said, turning in front of the mirror. She stopped and took in Grace's dress. "And I love that on you."

"Well, that didn't take long," Grace said with a laugh. "We even have time to stop by the coffee shop."

"Good. I could go for a brownie." Charlotte returned to her dressing room.

Once Charlotte was behind the curtain, Grace rushed across the shop to the counter. She scanned a display of earrings, then pointed to a pair of dangly gold ones featuring disks of various sizes. They would look great with her sister's new dress. "I want to buy those for Charlotte," she whispered. "But it's a secret."

Sophie smiled with a finger to her lips, then removed the earrings from the display.

Grace hurried back to her changing room, laughing to herself. It was so much fun surprising Charlotte with an unexpected gift.

Sophie had already rung up Charlotte's dress by the time Grace came out.

Charlotte was idly browsing a display of sunglasses, now and then trying on a pair.

Grace paid for her purchases, and the two of them said goodbye to Sophie, with promises to come back soon.

"I love that store," Charlotte said as they walked to the Dragonfly.

"Me too," Grace said.

Angel smiled when they entered the coffee shop. "I'm enjoying the retreat," she told them. "It's been so inspiring."

"I'm so glad to hear it," Grace said.

After Angel filled their coffee and dessert orders, they sat down at a table next to the window.

Charlotte leaned over and groped around in her shopping bag.

"Is something wrong?" Grace asked. While her sister was distracted, she pulled the earring box out of her pocket and put it close to Charlotte's place setting.

Charlotte sat up, a small box in her hand. "I couldn't resist." As she handed it to Grace, her gaze fell on the box near her mug. She burst into laughter. "Aren't we a pair?"

Grace opened the box, discovering beautiful crystal and blue beaded earrings. They would go perfectly with her new dress. "We sure are," she said. She reached for Charlotte's hand and gave it a squeeze. "Two peas in a pod."

April

April kicked off her sneakers and pushed her toes into the warm sand. She could hardly believe she was at the beach in January. She went down to the water, enjoying the effort it took to walk in loose sand. Every muscle stretching, awakening.

Like me. She stopped and held out her arms in sheer joy, turning her face to the sun. The worries about the future, the twinges in her body, the grief and regret of the past—they all dissolved in the sparkling sea air.

If only she could capture this moment and put it in a jar to keep it forever. But since that wasn't possible, she allowed it to imprint on her senses.

She also needed to come to the beach more often, at least once a year. Even if it was a four-hour drive from Asheville to Charleston.

Noticing that Shelby had stopped to wait for her, April got moving again. With each step toward the water, her heart beat a little faster. Owen and Trevor stood at the edge, casting lines into the water. Then Owen turned and waved. Even from a distance, she could see his grin.

Now she wanted to run. But that wasn't a good idea. After all, tumbling into the sand wasn't a very graceful look. April waved back, then continued steadily on her path until she joined Owen. "How's the fishing?" she asked.

"Not bad," he said, still wearing that attractive grin. His hat was pulled low and he wore sunglasses, but that smile said it all. He was happy to see her.

"I'm so glad we made the trip down here," April said. She glanced back at her friends. Jamie was working on her painting, and Dawn was writing in a notebook. "My friends are obviously inspired by the scenery here."

"How about you?" he asked.

April laughed. "I'm inspired too. Happy to be alive." He didn't know about her battle yet, she remembered.

But he seemed to take the remark in stride. "Me too." He inhaled deeply. "I was just thinking that I don't get to the beach often enough."

"So was I. Of course, it's an effort from where I live." April crossed her arms against the strong sea breeze. Her toes were getting chilly on the wet, packed sand, but she ignored them. When they turned blue, she would do something about it.

As if he were reading her mind, he glanced down and raised his brows. "Bare feet in January?"

She wiggled her toes. "As long as I can still move them, I'm good."

"Give me a few more minutes, and I'll come sit with you," Owen said. "We're almost ready for a break."

"Okay, I'll see you soon." April left him to his fishing and, noticing that Shelby and Trevor were still talking, she strolled up the beach. Ah, the sun-warmed sand felt great on her frozen feet.

When she returned, Jamie and Dawn were so absorbed in what they were doing that they barely glanced up.

April spread the other blanket and stretched out on it, wiggling until the sand cradled her body. The sun's heat, the cries of seagulls, and the wash of the waves combined to lull her to sleep.

A while later, when she opened her eyes, Owen and Shelby were looming over her. She sat up with a yawn. "Hi."

"You seemed so comfortable that I hated to disturb you," Shelby said. "But I didn't want you to get burned either." She handed April a bottle of sunscreen.

"Good call. Thanks." April popped the lid and applied some lotion to her face and forearms. The rest of her body was covered up, and her feet had a protective coating of sand. It would be difficult to remove all the sand before putting her shoes on again. Oh well, sand in her socks was a small price to pay.

Owen settled on a low chair nearby and dug through a tote bag. He pulled out a thermos and a few cups. "Want coffee?"

"No thanks," April said. She sat with her knees up, sipping from a water bottle.

Trevor accepted a cup of coffee as well as cookies from the container Dawn passed around.

"Charlotte made these," Dawn said.

Owen took a couple of cookies as well.

The group relaxed with their snacks, watching the waves roll in and people occasionally walk by. One young man tossed a disc for his dog, who leaped up to grab it in midair.

Owen asked April if she'd like to take a walk.

"I'd love to," she said, standing up and brushing off the loose sand. A walk on the beach. What a classic romantic activity.

But as they strolled along the edge of the water, the atmosphere was more friendly than romantic. They chatted about fishing, other visits to the beach, and pointed out various seabirds to each other.

"When are you leaving Magnolia Harbor?" April asked. "The retreat ends tomorrow."

Owen scratched the back of his neck. "Well, we were thinking about packing up and leaving tomorrow. But we might hang around." He gave her a crooked grin. "I'm not in a rush to go home."

Me either. But April only smiled, not sure if she was one of the reasons he wanted to linger. "It's a whole different world down here."

Owen gazed out to sea, his expression thoughtful. "Ellen loved the water. We used to spend many family vacations at the beach."

Ellen was Owen's late wife. He hadn't said much about her, beyond a brief mention that she'd died about five years before.

But now April felt she knew him well enough to ask, "What happened?"

With his gaze still on the ocean, he said, "She had breast cancer. Stage four. It took her quickly."

His words struck April like a blow. She actually felt herself hunch over in pain. "I'm so sorry," she managed to say.

Thankfully, he started walking again, giving her time to organize her tangled thoughts and emotions. She truly felt sorrow for Owen and Ellen. That disease—her disease—was a horrible one. At the same time, she was still fragile enough that seeing or hearing the word *cancer* caused a cascade of post-traumatic reactions.

April hadn't told Owen about her battle with the disease because she was afraid of scaring him off. He'd already lost his wife prematurely. But to find out that his wife had died of breast cancer was almost unfathomable. Why in the world would Owen risk a relationship with April, a breast cancer survivor? What if she had a relapse? She was nowhere near the five-year mark, the first optimistic milestone.

Surely he never wanted to go through that again.

Not that they were embarking on a relationship. What was this, their third encounter? Were they even close enough for her to mention her ordeal? April realized that it didn't matter. In another day or two, they'd go their separate ways and it would be over. She exhaled, allowing her mind to empty. *Stay in the present.*

Owen took her arm, pointing to something in the sea. "It's a humpback whale. I heard that people spotted one out here earlier this week."

At first April only saw a disturbance on the water's surface, a line of churning white. Then a huge whale arced out of the ocean, followed by a display of his tail. He breached a second time and rolled over, moving gracefully for such a large creature.

April and Owen stood close together, enthralled.

This was certainly a moment to remember.

22

Grace

The front doorbell chimed precisely at eight o'clock the next morning.

Grace, who was on her way to the kitchen, detoured to the front door.

Nina Briscoe, renowned stylist, stood on the front porch. Despite the early hour, her shoulder-length blonde hair and her subtle makeup were impeccable. She smiled, revealing gleaming teeth. "Good morning. You must be Grace. So nice to meet you." Her Southern accent was charming.

"That's right. Please come in." Grace stood back to let the woman enter. "Welcome to the Magnolia Harbor Inn."

Nina walked inside, pulling two roller bags behind her. She glanced around the foyer, her blue eyes wide with appreciation. "What a lovely old place. I can't believe I haven't stayed here before."

Grace bit back a thrilled exclamation. A mention from Nina would be incredible publicity for the inn. "We're so excited that you could visit us today. And please do come back and stay with us sometime." Grace escorted her to the music room. "This is where you can set up. Breakfast is in the dining room if you'd like to join us."

The stylist parked her bags and studied the room. "I'll be there a little later. I'd like to get situated first."

Grace made one final effort to ensure that her very important guest was comfortable. "Would you like coffee? I can bring you a tray."

"No thanks. I'll wait." Nina unzipped a case and appeared lost in thought.

Grace hurried to the dining room, eager to tell Charlotte that Nina had arrived. She found her sister placing platters of perfectly golden waffles on the buffet table. Toppings included heated jugs of real maple syrup, dishes of creamy butter, and assorted fruit. There were also platters of sausage links and bacon.

"Nina's here," Grace said. "I wonder what she thought of me."

Charlotte gave her a puzzled look. "That you're beautiful." Her lips quirked in a teasing smile. "For your age."

Grace gently bumped her younger sister's shoulder. "Rub it in, why don't you?" She moved aside so Charlotte could rearrange the plates. "But don't you think Nina views everyone like a project? Thinks about tweaks to make them look better?"

"You mean how I regard a pile of vegetables and imagine a salad? Maybe." Charlotte ran her hands over her spotless apron. "Breakfast is ready. Now we need people to eat it all."

As if on cue, the clatter of footsteps sounded in the foyer, accompanied by laughter and voices. Next the front door opened and Grace heard Winnie's distinctive voice.

"They're right on time," Grace said. "I'm going to grab a cup of coffee and get out of the way." She and Charlotte both stood near the table, ready to assist if any of their guests needed something.

Maya entered last, browsing through the selections. On her way to the table with a plate, she stopped to talk to the sisters. "Things are looking up," she said, her dark eyes sparkling. "That's all I can say right now."

Joy sparked in Grace's heart. "That's wonderful news. I'm so glad."

"Me too," Charlotte said. She held up crossed fingers. "We're rooting for you."

Maya smiled. "I really appreciate it." At the table, she took a seat beside April, who had a slight sunburn on her nose.

"Nina said she'd be in later, so I suppose we can go ahead and eat." Grace picked up a plate and chose a waffle, strawberries, and two sausage links, then doused everything with warm syrup.

Grace sat on the other side of Maya. Charlotte went to the opposite end, sitting between Paisley and Angel. Jamie, Shelby, and Dawn were chatting about something that provoked a lot of laughter.

"I was telling Maya about the beach," April said. "We saw a humpback whale."

"Oh, that is special," Grace said. When she lived in Charleston, she had spent a lot of time at the beach, even keeping a list of the wildlife, birds, and amphibians she spotted.

April set down her fork. "Yes, it was." Emotions warred on her face. She glanced around as if checking to see if anyone was listening. "Except I found out that Owen's wife died of breast cancer."

"Hold on," Maya said. "Who is Owen? Someone close?"

"No, not exactly." April bit her lip. "I'm sorry. I always assume everyone knows everything. I met Owen at The Tidewater. We went to trivia night, and then yesterday, I saw him fishing at Folly Beach."

"I remember noticing him at dinner," Grace said. "Good for you, dating already."

"All you ladies are fast workers," Maya said. "And I mean that in the best possible way." She sipped her coffee. "So Owen is a widower."

"Yes. His wife died about five years ago." Without seeming to realize it, April put a hand to her chest. "She had an aggressive form of breast cancer."

It all came together for Grace. Dawn and Jamie had arranged for April to have the Buttercup Suite with its private bath, and they'd told Grace that their friend needed cheerful surroundings right now. But Grace remained silent. A bout with cancer was April's news to tell.

"And you're worried Owen might not want to take that risk again?" Maya asked.

Grace focused on her breakfast, content to let Maya take the lead.

"Yes, that's exactly it. I haven't told him about my battle." She gave Grace a tight smile. "I have a good prognosis, but of course you never know."

"Are you going to see him again?" Maya asked.

April lifted her hands and let them drop. "I don't know. He said he might be leaving today. We live hours apart from each other." She lowered her voice. "But if I do hear from him, when do I tell him?"

"Whenever you feel comfortable," Maya said. "And since this is bothering you, I think maybe sooner rather than later."

"You're right," April said. "If he asks me out again, which may never happen, I'll tell him. Then he can choose whether or not to see me. Thanks, Maya. I feel so much better having a clear path." She pushed back from the table. "And on that note, I'm going to get seconds. These waffles are incredible."

Maya exchanged glances with Grace. "I'm always glad when my advice helps."

"Me too. It's such a responsibility," Grace said, thinking of how guests often confided in her about their struggles. "So what's on the agenda today?"

"The class will be creating dream boards while Nina holds individual appointments," Maya answered. "The hairstylists and other therapists are arriving after lunch. This evening, everyone will present their boards, and then we'll do a group photograph."

"That will be a great keepsake," Grace said. She could frame her picture and hang it on the wall of the inn for others to enjoy.

Nina entered the room and strolled over to the table.

Maya rose, and the two women embraced.

"Let me introduce you," Maya said.

"I've met Grace," Nina said with a warm smile. She held out a hand to April. "Hi, I'm Nina."

"I'm April Frederick." She shook Nina's hand. "Nice to meet you."

"Same here. Don't you have a lovely complexion? Like roses and cream." Nina made the rounds, greeting each woman with a compliment.

Grace had the feeling the consultant was carefully taking them in, no doubt formulating ideas for the styling sessions later.

As the ladies moved toward the living room under Maya's urging, Grace helped Charlotte clear the dishes and buffet table. Then they replenished the coffee and hot water urns. They left out the bowl of fruit and a big dish of yogurt for a snack.

The sisters arrived in the living room in time to hear Jamie whisper, "We're actually going to make posters? With markers and pictures from magazines?"

The long tables Maya had set up were strewn with stacks of magazines, glue sticks, markers, and scissors. Each woman had a big white piece of poster board to work with.

Maya evidently overheard Jamie's comments, but she didn't seem to take offense. "This exercise often seems like something children might do at school. But give it a try. I guarantee you'll enjoy it."

"What are we supposed to put on the boards?" Judith asked.

"Think of the dream board as a visual representation of your North Star goal, your achievements, and the steps you are taking toward your goal," Maya replied. "And show the outcome of your goal, what your life will look like when you reach it."

"Do you have a sample board to show us?" Shelby asked, a crease appearing between her brows. "I want to do it right."

"There is no right or wrong way," Maya said. "The boards can be plain or fancy, creative or crazy, whatever you want. These are for you to help you stay on track with your goals. And to visualize your life when you achieve them."

Dawn put up a hand. "Like when I get a book published?"

"Yes," Maya said. "That is a very concrete image."

Grace and Charlotte found spots at a table, and soon the room was filled with the sound of people rustling through magazines and chatting as they began designing their dream boards. April worked next to Shelby, both intent on the pictures they were gluing to their posters.

Jamie was the first to go for a consultation with Nina. After about forty-five minutes, she returned, posing in the doorway with arms wide. "Ta-da." Nina had applied delicate, flattering cosmetics, and Jamie looked lovely.

The other women made admiring comments.

"Nina showed me how to apply this makeup," Jamie said. "So I can do it myself. She said my hair was nice but needs a little more layering."

"You're next, Dawn," Maya said, consulting the list.

Dawn turned over her poster. "Nobody peek while I'm gone."

"We won't," Jamie called, leafing through a magazine. After a moment, she tossed it aside and picked up a set of markers.

The artist was drawing her own pictures, Grace guessed. That made sense.

"Look at this." Charlotte held up a magazine for Grace to see. "It's our inn." The magazine was a regional one, and they had featured the Magnolia Harbor Inn the previous summer.

"Oh, I need to use a picture from that," Grace said. Between them, they decided on who would get which picture. Grace pasted hers right in the center of her poster. Everything else in her life would radiate out from there.

Dawn returned, with new makeup that made her already large eyes stand out even more.

"Wow," Jamie said. She pulled out her phone. "I'm sending a picture to your husband." She took several shots while Dawn posed, laughing.

"Nina told me to send you in next, April," Dawn said.

"Just a second," April said, cutting a picture out of a magazine. "I want to glue this on first."

Dawn came over to the table to admire April's poster. She put a hand to her heart. "Your board is gorgeous."

Shelby and Jamie edged closer to see.

"You think so? It's not too much?" April turned to Grace. "What do you think?"

Grace peered over April's shoulder. The pictures April had chosen included a pretty home surrounded by gardens, children around a Christmas tree, and most touching, a bride in a white dress and veil. April was definitely expressing her heart's desires. "I love it," Grace said around the lump in her throat.

"Thanks." April applied glue to the back of a picture and placed it on the poster. "This will only take a sec."

Grace saw it was a photograph showing a smiling doctor with a female patient. She had to turn away or else embarrass herself by bursting into tears.

"Check out mine," Shelby said. She had glued a similar picture of a bride in the corner of her poster. Most of hers was filled with ideas for her business and a home of her own.

"We're going to get there, just you wait," April said as she embraced Shelby.

It was apparent to Grace that they had bonded over their desire for marriage.

April released her friend. "I'd better scoot." Then her phone rang in her pocket. She checked the caller, her eyes wide. The call was short, and she shivered with excitement as she tucked the phone away.

"Guess who has a dinner date tonight. The perfect occasion to wear my new dress."

"With Owen?" Dawn asked.

April nodded.

"You're on your way to your goal," Shelby crowed. "Go, April."

April glanced at Grace, the excitement tinged with doubt. "I hope it goes well. Tonight I'm going to tell Owen about my diagnosis."

Grace sent April an encouraging smile. "If he's right for you, it will all work out," she said, meaning it.

April deserved someone who would love her without reservation.

Shelby

Shelby regarded her finished dream board with satisfaction. In her new business, she would strive to create peaceful perfection for her customers. To underscore that, she wrote words in glitter pen around the inspiring images of well-organized interiors. *Home. Rest. Relax. Restore.*

That was the point, right? An organized home provided the freedom to enjoy it. She knew that from firsthand experience. When her town house was a mess, she couldn't relax.

And that thought had led her to another area of her dream board. She wanted her own home someday. She didn't care if it was big and fancy, as long as she had enough room for a garden and some space to spread out. The picture of the rose-covered cottage was right next to a picture of her dream wedding dress. Shelby liked old-fashioned styles, with long sleeves and a full skirt.

"You're up, Shelby," April said, returning to her seat. She patted her hair. "What do you think?" Nina had changed April's part and adorned her face with light cosmetics.

"You look adorable," Shelby said.

"Thank you." April glanced over at Shelby's poster. "Oh, I like the glitter pens. I'm going to use those on mine."

Shelby handed her the package of pens. "I'll be back soon." As she left the table and headed toward the music room, she felt eager and a little afraid. What was Nina going to tell her? As instructed, she had worn her usual makeup.

"Hey, Shelby," Nina said when she entered the room. "Please stand there." She pointed to a place on the rug. "How are you?"

"I'm fine." Shelby moved to the designated spot. "But a little nervous."

"Don't be," Nina said as she circled her, studying her from head to toe. "You're beautiful. And you're doing a lot of things right."

Shelby felt her shoulders slump. "You mean I'm not a disaster?" She'd seen a few makeover shows where the client was torn apart. And how humiliating would it be if an organizer couldn't even put herself together?

Nina chuckled. "No, of course not." She reached out and touched Shelby's hair. "I think this needs to be a bit shorter, with a few more layers. Then it will fall into place and stay that way all day."

"Really? I always have to wrestle with it." Shelby's shoulder-length hair was thick and glossy, one of her prides. But it had a natural curl that tended to get out of control in humidity.

"We work with your hair, not against it," Nina said. "Please have a seat."

Shelby sat on a stool.

Nina studied her face before cleaning off the makeup.

"What's the verdict?" Shelby asked.

"Not bad," Nina said. "But I'm going to go with a copper, brown, and peach palette for you. Pink doesn't do enough for your coloring."

Good to know. Shelby had always gravitated toward pink lipstick and blush. And she used black mascara and eyeliner, like almost everyone else.

"I love doing this," Nina said as she deftly worked on Shelby's makeup. "I feel like an artist."

"You are," Shelby said. Nina had done an impressive job on her friends.

"Thank you," Nina responded. "Are you enjoying the retreat?"

"Yes, it's been great," Shelby said. "It's motivated me to start a new business. Organizing."

Nina cocked her head. "Oh, that's interesting. I could use an organizer in my studio. When I'm busy, it gets completely out of hand."

Shelby's heart skipped a beat. This was an opportunity to sell her services—if she had the courage. But Nina Briscoe was nationally known. Why would she hire Shelby?

Why not? Shelby gritted her teeth in determination, then realizing what she was doing, commanded her face muscles to relax. "Tell me about your needs."

As Nina continued to apply makeup, she described the studio and the closets full of cosmetics as well as clothing and other accessories. "I sell a fashion line. When I dress people for important interviews, it's often easier to choose their outfits." She picked through a tray of lipstick samples. "But I also do personal shopping with clients after we do closet purges."

"Do some of these clients need to reorganize their closets?" Shelby asked.

Nina laughed. "They certainly do. I recommend that they start from scratch and add pieces slowly. A good system helps them see what they have."

Not only was the stylist a possible customer, but she might provide referrals. "Do you mind if I contact you in the next several weeks?" Shelby asked. "I'd appreciate it if you could give me referrals. I'll send you a link so you can see my work." She needed to scramble to set up a website with photographs, but she felt that she was up to the task.

"Please feel free," Nina said. "And I mean that. I had a start-up business once myself, you know." She gently placed her hands on Shelby's shoulders. "Take a peek."

Shelby turned on the stool to face the mirror. Her mouth dropped open. The new palette brought out her coloring, and even her freckles looked better. She bent closer. Maybe they weren't so bad after all.

"Your freckles are cute. Trust me." Nina slid the makeup samples she'd used on Shelby into a small bag. "So many women try to conform to a cookie-cutter beauty. But distinctive features make us unique. So rock those freckles."

Shelby smiled at her reflection. She was going to take that advice to heart.

Late that afternoon, Shelby enjoyed a long bubble bath, thinking over the day. After the makeup sessions, Nina had presented advice on dressing for specific body types over lunch. Later two hairstylists, a massage therapist, and an aromatherapist had arrived.

A stylist had cut Shelby's hair to Nina's specifications, and Shelby had gotten a relaxing massage.

Then she had a session with the aromatherapist, who blended a combination of grapefruit, orange, and bergamot for Shelby.

"It's not magic," the therapist explained. "Aromas affect our physical bodies. We can't control what everything smells like, but we can enhance our personal environments." She dabbed oil on Shelby's wrist. "This combination boosts confidence."

Between the new makeup and hairstyle, the massage, and the essential oils, Shelby felt like a brand-new person. She was ready to return home and take on the world.

Noting the time, Shelby dried off and reapplied her makeup using the samples from Nina. Shelby was relieved that the process was quite simple. She didn't have the time or patience for multiple layers of paint. Once she was done with her face, she went to the closet to retrieve her new dress.

Thankfully for her budget, the session about dressing for specific body types had confirmed that this style worked on Shelby. As a volunteer model during the class, Shelby learned to emphasize her waist and make sure skirts weren't too long or pants too wide. Both swamped her small stature.

Shelby slipped into heels, then checked her appearance. *Not bad.* A last smooth of her hair and she was ready.

In the second-floor hallway below, April, Dawn, and Jamie were emerging from their rooms.

"Shelby," April called, "you're right on time."

"I thought I was going to be late," Shelby said, hurrying down the last few steps. "I soaked in the bathtub until I was a prune." She was aware of the three admiring faces turned her way.

"You look amazing," Dawn said. "Love the haircut."

"So do all of you," Shelby said. "This is so much fun, isn't it?"

"Yes," April said. "It feels like my prom night or something."

"Well, you do have a date," Jamie said with mock annoyance as they moved toward the stairs. She glanced at Dawn. "Too bad our husbands are so far away."

"We'll tell them they have to take us out next weekend," Dawn said. She twitched her new dress into place. "I plan on wearing this outfit a lot."

"What about you, Shelby?" Jamie asked. "Are you seeing Trevor tonight?"

"I don't know," Shelby said. Her mouth fell open. "I haven't checked my phone all day." She had shut it off to avoid possible communication with Devon. She hesitated on the stairs. "I left it in my room."

"Check it after the photo," April said. "I hear Grace herding people into place."

In the lobby, people were milling around, with Grace and Maya trying to arrange them in some semblance of order. Perfume and laughter filled the air.

Everyone looks spectacular, Shelby thought as she joined the chaos.

Maya used a tripod to capture the photo, which necessitated some running back and forth and test shots. She wanted two pictures, one with the dream boards and one without. Finally, they captured several photographs that she said were perfect.

"Please gather in the living room for social hour," Grace said.

The women began moving that way in a group.

"What time is Owen coming to get you?" Dawn asked April.

"In about an hour," April said.

"Good." Jamie slipped her arm through April's. "You have time for a glass of wine."

Shelby headed for the stairs. "I'm going to get my phone. Be right back." She couldn't wait to see if Trevor had called. She really hoped so.

She was halfway up the stairs when an automobile's throaty roar sounded out in the driveway. Shelby knew that rumbling engine all too well. Holding her breath, she clattered down the steps and opened the front door. The sight of the familiar sports car made her knees go weak. She had to lean against the doorjamb to remain upright.

Devon Smith had just arrived.

24

Shelby

Shelby shut the door, her heart pounding. What should she do? She was torn between waiting for Devon to come inside and checking her phone, as she had planned.

But she liked Trevor too much to ignore him, if he had called. She dashed for the stairs and ran the two flights up to her room. Devon could cool his heels anyway. What kind of message did it send for her to linger by the front door?

Desperation. And Shelby was not desperate, not anymore. Panting for breath, she unlocked the Wisteria Loft Suite and ducked inside. She shut the door with a sense of barring it against any intruders.

This is a good opportunity, a little voice told her. Standing in front of the full-length mirror, noting her flushed cheeks, she realized that her new resolutions were being put to the test. She raised her chin. *Confidence. Hold out for what I really want.*

Shelby grabbed her phone from the bureau and plugged it into the wall. She turned it on. Yes, she had a message from Trevor. He wanted to see her tonight. They weren't leaving today after all. They would be in town until Monday.

Her fingers hovered over the screen. What should she say? She had to see Devon, she supposed. Although she could stay up here, refusing to go downstairs. But that would be cowardly. She needed to talk to him and put the relationship to rest.

The room phone rang.

With her heart kicking into overdrive, she snatched it up. "Hello?"

"Shelby?" Winnie asked. "There's a young man here to see you."

"I know," Shelby said. "Tell him I'll be down in a few minutes. Thank you." After hanging up, she sank onto the foot of the bed and dialed Trevor.

He picked up right away. "Hey. I was wondering if you got my message."

"I just did." She forced a laugh. "I had my phone off all day."

"It happens. Would you like to have dinner? It's kind of short notice now. I understand if you're busy . . ." His voice was warm and deep. It enveloped Shelby like a blanket, offering comfort and kindness.

Shelby winced, wanting so much to say yes. But she had to face Devon one last time. "I'm sorry, but something came up." She heard the tentative note in her voice, as if she were fibbing.

"Okay. Well, it was good getting to know—"

"Hold on. I mean it. I'm not giving you the brush-off." She was going to have to tell him the truth. "My ex-boyfriend just arrived. Without asking me first. So I've got to talk to him and convince him that it's over." She hunched her shoulders and whispered, "I would much rather be having dinner with you."

Trevor whistled. "Whoa. Are you okay with seeing him? If not, I could send him packing."

What a gentleman. "He's not dangerous. Just selfish." She hesitated before saying, "It's Devon Smith."

Trevor was silent for a moment. "Devon Smith, as in the driver?" He fell silent again, and even over the phone line, Shelby could sense his wheels turning. There wasn't anyone who lived in the Charlotte area who hadn't seen Devon on television.

"Yeah, that Devon," Shelby said. "I should go down and talk to him."

"All right. Listen, if you need me, let me know, okay? I'll be around."

"Thank you," she said. "I appreciate it."

"Take care."

Shelby felt cast adrift when Trevor hung up, as if he offered a lifeline. That was interesting. They'd known each other less than a week, yet she knew she could count on him. She picked up the angel wing shell he'd given her and tucked it into her handbag.

It was time to face the music.

When Shelby came down the stairs, she saw Devon standing in the foyer. He was examining a painting on the wall. His back was to her, and she paused to study him. Still as handsome as ever, with broad shoulders and tousled dark hair curling onto his collar. He was wearing a leather jacket, jeans, and boots. Even from a distance, she caught a whiff of his expensive aftershave.

Perhaps sensing her presence, he whirled around. His eyes were the same too, deep and dark. They lit with joy at seeing her. "Shelby." He took her in from head to toe. "You look gorgeous." He sounded slightly surprised, as if he'd expected to find her in a disheveled, tearstained heap.

Shelby straightened her shoulders and strutted the rest of the way, just as she and April had practiced.

Devon held out his arms as she approached, evidently ready to swoop in for a kiss.

But she stayed out of reach. "What are you doing here?"

"I came to see you," he said.

Shelby crossed her arms. "But I told you it was over." She spoke in a low voice so the people in the adjacent rooms wouldn't overhear.

A series of expressions crossed his face, almost as if he were trying to decide on an approach. Finally, he glanced over his shoulder. "What do you say we get out of here? I have a lot to talk to you about. And this isn't the best place. There are too many people around."

Shelby was tempted to refuse, but then she thought better of it.

Why not hear him out? It wasn't like she would change her mind. And letting him have his say would be the decent thing to do, even if he hadn't been exactly honorable.

"Fine. But I don't want to go anywhere local." Her face burned at the thought of running into Trevor or Owen or any of the other new friends she'd made in Magnolia Harbor.

"I have an idea." Devon jingled his car keys. "Let's try Le Crabe Fou in Charleston. It's supposed to be good."

"The chef at this inn used to work there," Shelby said, seizing on the neutral topic. "She's awesome."

"So you'll go with me?" He gave her his trademark smile. "I'll be good. Promise."

"You'd better." Shelby shrugged. "Sure, I'd like to check it out. But I want to get back at a reasonable hour. The restaurant and that's it. No clubbing."

Devon made a face. He'd accused her of being a spoilsport more than once in the past. But this time he quickly amended his expression. "Whatever you want. Let's hit the road."

"I need to get my coat," she said. "And tell someone where I'm going."

"Why?" he asked.

"They're my friends, and they'll worry," Shelby explained.

Devon pursed his lips but didn't comment. "I'll call ahead for a reservation." He pulled out his phone.

As Shelby went upstairs for her coat, she noticed him taking a selfie in front of a portrait on the wall. *Typical.* She'd have to make sure he didn't take any pictures of her during their dinner.

Shelby retrieved her coat, then stopped in the living room to talk to April and the others.

"Would you like a glass of wine?" Grace asked, standing near the buffet table. "And would your guest?"

"No thanks," Shelby said. "We'll be back later. We're headed to Le Crabe Fou."

Charlotte gave her a thumbs-up at hearing the restaurant name.

April came over, concern etched on her brow. "You're going out with Devon?"

Shelby nodded. "He wants to talk to me, and I feel like it will give us closure."

Her new friend hugged her, whispering, "Listen to him. That will tell you all you need to know."

"I will," Shelby promised. "But I have no intention of going back to him."

April's expression was grave. "You need to do what's right for you." The subtext was loud and clear. April wouldn't judge her if she did make up with Devon.

"You're the best." Shelby gave the others a smile and a wave before hurrying out. She wanted to get the whole thing over with. The realization jolted her. Before the incident a week ago, she'd savored every minute with Devon. They weren't exactly plentiful, so she'd grabbed on to them like precious gems threatening to slip through her fingers. Now she'd learned that the gems were cheap imitations.

"I'm ready," she said when she entered the lobby, slipping her handbag strap over one shoulder.

Standing near the front door, Devon sprang into action and opened it for her. He even bowed slightly. "After you."

She felt as though he were playing the role of devoted suitor. What would happen when she didn't stay on script?

Shelby smiled. They were about to find out.

April

April felt mixed emotions as she watched Shelby leave the inn. She'd caught a glimpse of Devon Smith and saw firsthand how devastatingly attractive he was. In addition to his good looks, he had the charisma of a film star. No wonder Shelby had agreed to date him. Most young women would leap at the chance.

"I hope Shelby will be okay," Dawn said, coming to sit beside April on a sofa. "My guess is that Devon is hard to resist."

"I know," April said. "I was just thinking that. He's the type who sweeps a girl off her feet."

Dawn sipped her wine, thoughtful. "Our Shelby deserves better. Like Trevor, for example. Now there's a nice young man to bring home to Mama."

"Agreed," April said. She checked the wall clock. "Owen will be here soon. I'd better go upstairs and get ready."

"I can tell that he's a keeper too," Dawn said. "Believe me, I dated my share of frogs back in the day."

Dawn had a wonderful husband, so April decided to go with her judgment. But that didn't solve the problem of her illness. Owen might not be up to caring for another woman who might have a relapse.

April gritted her teeth. She had to do the right thing and let the chips fall where they may. The idea of hiding her bout with breast cancer was tempting, but it was wrong. And there was something special about Owen. Otherwise, she wouldn't bother.

Owen had arrived by the time April was descending the stairs. His whole face lit up when he saw her. "You look lovely."

She couldn't hold back a grin. "Thank you."

At the bottom of the stairs, Owen held out his hand for her to take. He was such a gentleman.

He also helped her into the truck, apologizing that it wasn't a fancier ride. "But I did clean it today," he said.

"It's fine," April said, settling into the seat. She thought it was sweet that he worried about details like that. But of course he had a truck. How else would he transport the fishing boat?

Owen hopped into the driver's seat, and they were off.

As they drove through the quiet town, April wondered how Shelby was doing with Devon. She pictured them racing along the highway in his sports car, and her heart clenched. But he was a professional driver, she reminded herself.

"A celebrity from back home checked into The Tidewater this afternoon," Owen said. "A stock car racer."

"Really?" April decided to play dumb since it wasn't her place to reveal Shelby's relationship with Devon. But how incredibly awkward for Trevor and Devon to be staying at the same inn. She'd have to give Shelby a heads-up in case Devon didn't mention it.

"Devon Smith." Owen chuckled. "Some of the young ladies who work there were mighty impressed."

April didn't know how to respond, so she remained silent.

Owen changed the subject and asked April about her day, and they talked about the retreat.

They arrived at the restaurant almost too soon. April enjoyed riding in the truck with Owen.

"I heard this was a good place," Owen said as he pulled into a parking spot at Turner's Lakeside Grill.

April glanced around the parking lot. Judging by the number of other vehicles, the assessment was right. The place was jammed.

Owen turned off the engine. "Stay put. I'm coming around."

Feeling like a fragile flower, April waited for him to open her door.

He assisted her down from the high seat, a process that was a little lacking in grace on her end.

"Whoops," she said with a laugh.

He laughed too, then ushered her toward the door, almost but not quite putting his arm around her shoulders.

April enjoyed his attention, but with every sweet gesture, her tension grew. She had to tell him about her diagnosis soon.

Inside the restaurant, the hostess seated them at a table near the window, where a flickering candle reflected in the glass. She handed them two long menus.

"I'll bet the view is great," Owen said, grinning at the young woman. "In the daytime."

She smiled. "It is. We're right on the water." She filled their water glasses. "Your server will be right with you. Enjoy."

Owen held up his water glass. "Cheers."

April copied him, and they clinked glasses. She took a sip. As she set the glass down, she wondered if she should bring it up now or wait until after they ate dinner.

Owen flipped through the menu, absorbed by the numerous listings. "They sure don't make it easy. But I'm thinking steak."

April scanned the listings. "And I'm thinking shrimp." This close to the coast, it was probably really fresh. And April loved fresh shrimp. She told Owen about the time in Florida when she'd bought shrimp right off the boat.

"Nothing like fresh. You'll have to come out with me sometime, and we'll catch our dinner." He rubbed a hand across the linen tablecloth.

"Of course, I'm talking a campfire and sitting on a log, not ambience like this."

"I like eating outdoors," April said. "Everything tastes better."

The server appeared and took their orders. Both chose sweet tea to drink.

A few minutes later, the server set a loaf of bread and a crock of butter in the middle of the table.

April groaned. "Oh my. I can't resist warm homemade bread."

"Me either," Owen said, slicing a piece for April.

As April buttered her bread, she made a decision. There was no way she could bring up a topic like cancer during dinner. It would ruin the meal and quite possibly their appetites. She didn't want to do that to Owen.

During the delicious dinner, the conversation roamed around in the way April liked best. They hopped from topic to topic, learning more about each other as they went. April gathered that Owen had a deep integrity, not only in his daily life but in his business too. He spoke of his commitment to quality and value for his clients.

In return, April shared how much she enjoyed helping young minds learn and grow. "They are all so precious. Each child is different, and I love seeing their personalities develop."

"You're probably everyone's favorite teacher," Owen said with a smile. "I had a couple of those myself."

"I'm inspired by the teacher I had in first grade." April waited for the next questions to come, as they so often did. Why didn't she have her own children, since she loved them so much? Why wasn't she married?

But Owen didn't ask. He sipped his sweet tea, seemingly content to mind his own business.

So April found herself confiding in him. "I always did want a family of my own," she said softly. "But after a broken engagement, I never found the right person. Now it's almost too late."

"I appreciate you sharing that with me. Everyone isn't as fortunate as Ellen and me. We met in high school, believe it or not." Owen sighed. "My two oldest boys had a rocky road. They're finally doing okay. Now I'm just waiting for Trevor to settle down, and then I can relax." He laughed, squeezing her hand and releasing it.

Later as they drank decaffeinated coffee and shared a piece of key lime pie for dessert, April was still thinking about his revelation. Owen and Ellen had basically been childhood sweethearts, so he'd had a long, happy marriage. Ellen had certainly left a big pair of shoes to fill. Not that she was sure she wanted to put them on, of course.

A tingle went up her spine. Now was the time. *Now or never.* "I have something to tell you."

"You have a secret husband stashed away?" Owen joked.

April didn't laugh.

"I'm sorry," he said. "Didn't mean to poke fun."

"No, I enjoy making light of things. It's how I get through life." She swallowed. "Anyway, what I want to say is this . . . I recently went through treatment for breast cancer."

His face creased with concern. "I'm so sorry." He put up a hand. "I don't want to intrude, but I'm listening if you want to talk."

April filled him in, mentioning that it had been diagnosed at a fairly early stage so the outlook was good. "I'm cautiously optimistic and determined to wring the last drop out of life." As though to demonstrate, she picked up her cup and drained it.

"Good for you. I'm right with you on that. If Ellen's illness taught me anything, it's to hold people close. No one knows how much time they have."

April nodded. She was almost overcome with relief at how well the conversation had gone. And her relief told her something significant. She was starting to care for Owen with a depth she hadn't felt for a very long time.

Owen reached for her hand across the table. "I want to keep the conversation going with you. See where it all leads." He appeared uncertain. "I hope you feel the same."

April squeezed his hand. "I absolutely do."

26

Shelby

As Devon raced down the highway in his powerful sports car, Shelby closed her eyes and gripped the edge of the leather seat. *Relax. He's a highly skilled driver.* But the reminder did nothing to quell her nerves. A vision of Trevor, his steady nature and calm demeanor, flashed into her mind.

"This is great," Devon said, moving over to pass a line of cars. "I love driving at night, a beautiful woman by my side." He glanced at her. "You do something different to your hair?"

Her spirits lifted at the compliment and the fact he had examined her closely enough to notice. But then she felt a rush of anger. Did he really think that one little compliment would smooth over what he had done to her?

"I just got a trim." Shelby turned to the window and stared at the dark landscape rushing by. No, she wasn't so easily won. Not anymore.

They drove another few miles in silence.

"There's something different about you," he said.

I grew a backbone. But she held back the tart rejoinder. "It's been an interesting trip," she said. "I decided to start a business."

"Really?" Devon sounded distracted. But they had reached the outskirts of Charleston, and maybe he was concentrating on the exit signs. He found the right one and peeled off, wheeling to a stop at the bottom of the ramp.

Shelby didn't bother to pursue the topic while he crawled along the city streets searching for the restaurant. They found it, then had to go past it to find a place to park.

With edgy sighs and muttered exclamations, Devon finally pulled into a parking garage.

Shelby knew he hated using garages because the spaces were too tight and cars were frequently damaged.

As she expected, he drove all the way up to the roof, where there were no other vehicles. As an extra precaution, he straddled two parking spaces.

Devon climbed out and waited for her to struggle out of the low-slung automobile. The winter wind tore at Shelby's hair and dress, making her shiver.

In silence, they walked to the elevator and rode down, Shelby holding her nose against stale smells. She shivered again in the chilly space.

"Are you cold, babe?" Devon moved close, slinging an arm around her shoulders.

Even though his touch was warm and familiar, Shelby stepped away. "Don't touch me."

He eyed her up and down, his complexion sallow in the glow of sodium lights. "You really are mad, aren't you?"

The door opened at ground level, which gave Shelby a moment to think. She walked out ahead of him toward the street. She wasn't going to have this conversation in a dank, dirty, freezing parking garage.

She spotted the Le Crabe Fou sign a block away and kept walking, leaving him to catch up. When he started to say something, she raised a hand. "Wait. I don't want to talk out here." She kept her gaze forward, sensing him stealing looks at her, obviously disconcerted by her regal attitude.

Well, being a friendly, lovable lapdog hadn't worked to keep his attention. Apparently, he only responded to mistreatment.

That thought made her steps hitch. Did she want to be that kind of woman? Absolutely not. *Sounds like something he needs to work out, maybe with a therapist.*

At the entrance, Shelby stood back and waited for him to open the door, then strode inside, her head high. The restaurant was small and intimate, the atmosphere hushed and the lighting low. Light jazz played over the sound system.

"Reservation for Smith," Devon told the hostess.

The hostess beamed as recognition dawned. "Devon Smith?"

He nodded.

The hostess tipped her head, a flirtatious gleam in her eyes. "I'm a big fan."

Devon appeared pained. "I'm so glad to hear it. But please, can you give us a little privacy tonight?"

The young woman's gaze shifted to Shelby, then away. "Of course," she said, her enthusiasm dimmed. "Follow me." She led them to a corner banquette, placed near a barrier holding luxurious plants.

Shelby slid onto the leather seat, moving toward the middle. She would have preferred to face Devon head-on, but this would have to do.

"Your server will be right with you," the hostess said, gazing at Devon while she set the menus down on the table.

Devon pushed a hand through his hair. "Thanks." He smiled at the hostess as he slid into the seat from the other side.

The woman finally walked away, glancing back at him over her shoulder.

Shelby's spirits sank with a thud. "You can't help yourself, can you?" As soon as she'd said it, she could have bitten off her own tongue. Even if it were true, she didn't need to come across like a jealous nag.

"What do you mean? I was being polite to a fan." His face settled into unhappy lines. "I'm here with you, Shelby. I don't care about anyone else."

She didn't respond, her silence the most adequate retort she could make.

His cheeks reddened. "But it's true," he protested. "Angelique didn't mean anything. Besides, *she* came on to *me*."

Shelby shook her head with regret. "I'm not buying it. Angelique wasn't the first, and she won't be the last." She shrugged. "I guess it goes with the territory of being a famous driver. I have no claim on you, so you can do whatever you want. But I don't have to be part of it."

To her surprise—and horror—Devon got out of the seat and dropped to his knees.

Diners around them turned to watch, curious. A couple of them pulled out phones, ready to take photographs or videos.

Devon put a hand to his heart, turning his best side to the cameras. "But you do have a claim, Shelby. A claim on my heart."

How awful that she noticed him posing. And how awful would it be to have this scene all over social media? To think that only a few weeks ago, Shelby had longed for a moment like this. In her daydreams, she imagined Devon making a dramatic declaration of love, admitting that she was the one for him.

But now, during the actual event, she was blushing in embarrassment, not delight. "Devon, please get up."

A young woman approached, braid swinging, notepad in hand. Their server. She stopped short when she saw Devon on the floor. "Oh, I'm sorry. Did I interrupt something?"

"No, you didn't," Shelby assured her. To Devon, she said, "Look, I found my phone." She held it up. "I thought it fell under the table."

An obviously disgruntled Devon stood and brushed off the knees of his jeans. He collapsed onto the leather seat and scooted over but not too close to Shelby. He flipped open the menu with an abrupt gesture, like a pouting child.

Or at least that was how Shelby saw it. She ignored Devon and addressed the server. "I'd like to have the seafood salad as an entrée, with parmesan peppercorn dressing on the side and iced tea to drink. Thank you."

Devon hastily ordered the filet mignon and iced tea. After the server left, he scowled at Shelby. "Thanks for making me look like a fool."

She wasn't responsible for that now or ever. "Were you seriously going to propose?" she asked, allowing skepticism to seep into her tone.

In answer, he ducked his head and fiddled with the silverware. Finally, he said, "I was trying to show you that I care. Since you don't seem to believe me."

Shelby remained silent for a moment. The memory of Angelique seemed to dance in the space between them. "I'm sorry." And she meant it. "Too little, too late. I'm over it."

"In a week? You got over me in a week?" Devon slumped back, arms folded. His lip curled. "I guess you didn't really care after all."

Shelby studied his face. Although she perceived how perfect he was in an objective way, she felt nothing. He might as well be a photograph in a magazine. "No, I cared." Her mind flashed to the days and nights of tears and pain. "I was devastated at first. But I healed." And now she wasn't willing to take the risk again. She didn't dare voice that last bit. If he saw any crack in her defenses, he would dig away with his wiles until he widened it.

The server brought their drinks and a basket of bread. "Your meals will be out shortly." She regarded Devon with wide eyes, obviously now in the know about his identity.

He gave her a small wave of acknowledgment and a wan smile.

"I have an idea," Shelby said after the server left. "Why don't we stay and have a nice dinner? We're not getting back together, but we can still be friends, right?"

With a moody stare, Devon swirled the glass of iced tea, making the cubes tinkle. Then he nodded. A moment later, he started giving her a blow-by-blow description of his last training session. As he talked, the animation returned to his face and body language.

Maybe someday he would grow up. He hadn't even asked about her new business, she realized. No, everything was always about Devon. Why hadn't she seen that before? Maybe she'd been blinded by the dazzle of his charisma.

Shelby inhaled a deep breath. She couldn't wait for this dinner to be over and to return to her real life.

A life full of good friends and new opportunities.

And perhaps something more with Trevor.

April

"This has been a wonderful evening," Owen said after signing the credit card slip. "I hate for it to end." He tucked the receipt inside the leather folder along with the pen.

April smiled. "I feel the same way."

After confiding in Owen, joy and well-being had flooded April, making her spirits soar. She felt as if she'd vaulted over a significant hurdle, one that had loomed large. She had told a date that she had cancer. And he hadn't run away screaming, even though he'd lost his wife to the exact same disease. The dream that seemed just out of reach was now a tiny bit closer to her grasp. Maybe her goal of a marriage and family was within the realm of possibility.

He helped April with her coat, then glanced at her footwear. "Are you up for an evening stroll? I noticed the lakeside path is paved."

"That sounds wonderful, and I can walk in these shoes." April peered out the window. The night was crisp, but the air was still, so being outside would be comfortable enough. Globe streetlights lit the path, giving plenty of visibility, and the moon was rising as well.

The moon. April stifled a laugh. Taking a moonlit walk was another romantic cliché often seen in personal ads. When Owen sent her a questioning look, she explained.

"So we're hitting all the clichés," he said. "Stroll on the beach, moonlit walk. I like traveling too."

She laughed, recognizing yet another commonly used phrase. "But in your boat," she added. "That's different."

Outside the restaurant, Owen held out his arm for her to take, and they ambled through the parking lot toward the path. "Speaking of my boat, would you like to go fishing tomorrow?"

Fishing wasn't something April had ever pursued, but it was an opportunity to spend more time with Owen. "Maybe. And I only say that because we're supposed to check out tomorrow morning. I came with Dawn and Jamie, so I need to leave when they do." But perhaps they would want to stay another night. She would ask them later.

"Let me know if you decide to stay," Owen said. "We're going home Monday now."

Taking their time, they wandered along the path, stopping now and then to gaze at the moon hovering over the water. A necklace of lights surrounded the lake, and April tried to pick out the Magnolia Harbor Inn.

April sighed. "It's so beautiful. And quiet." Besides an occasional passing car on the road, the only sound was the gentle lapping of water on the shore.

"And so are you," Owen said. Then he laughed. "Well, maybe not the second one."

Laughing too, she elbowed him. But her pulse had leaped up a notch. Had he really said she was beautiful?

"April." He gently turned her to face him. "May I kiss you?"

It had been ages since a man had asked to kiss her and not because she hadn't been kissed. They usually didn't ask permission. She laughed again. "Please do."

His kiss was tender and light. It was a token of affection more than an attempt to push things along. Owen was a gentleman through and through, a wonderful man in every way.

But as they headed toward the restaurant parking lot, a sense of anxiety gripped April. Was Owen wrong for her as a potential partner? But the kiss had been perfect. Or was she falling into her old pattern of shoving a man away before he could get too close? Memories of her broken engagement lingered at the edge of her mind.

She was so confused. And that was all she was sure about.

The phone in April's room rang as she was coming through the door. She rushed inside and answered.

"How did it go?" Dawn said without preamble.

"Why did you call me on this phone?" April asked, shrugging off her coat and setting her handbag on the dresser.

"I didn't want to interrupt you on your cell if you were still on your date," Dawn said. "Did you have a good time?"

"The short answer is yes." Misery twisted in April's stomach. "Until he kissed me."

"Why? Was it awful?" Dawn asked. "Wait. Don't answer that. We're coming over with snacks."

A few minutes later, Dawn and Jamie knocked, then barged through the unlocked door. Her friends had changed into casual clothes.

"We brought milk and cookies," Jamie said, setting a tray on a side table.

"And I have chocolate." Dawn displayed a huge candy bar, then ripped off the wrapper.

"You two are the best." April took off her shoes. "Let me go change." In the bathroom, she slipped out of her dress and tugged on pajamas. Then, barefoot, she joined the other two. "Hold on," she said, curling up in a chair. "We're missing someone. Is Shelby back yet?"

"I believe so," Dawn said. "I think I heard that sports car roar up the drive."

Jamie waved her hand as if burned. "Devon Smith. Wow." She filled three glasses with milk and passed them around.

April hopped up. "I'm going to call her room."

Shelby answered right away, sounding pensive but not upset.

"Want milk and cookies and girl talk?" April asked. "Dawn and Jamie are here in my room."

"Sounds good," Shelby said. "I'll be there in a minute."

When April hung up, she turned to her friends. "She's on the way."

"Good," Jamie said, settling on a chair with a flounce. "I love Shelby."

"What do you think about staying another night?" Dawn asked April, then sat down on the love seat. "Jamie and I would like to spend more time on our projects. Grace said we could have the rooms."

"The weather is supposed to be good," Jamie said. "I'd love to do some painting on the shore before heading back into our normal chaos."

And April could go fishing with Owen after all. Or not. "Sure, I'm up for that." She returned to her chair.

Someone knocked on the door.

"Come in," April called. "It's open."

Shelby entered, also dressed in casual clothing. "Hey, ladies."

"We just decided to stay another night," Jamie said. "Why don't you join us?"

"That sounds nice," Shelby said. "I think I will if my room is still available."

"Great," Dawn said. "So tell us what happened."

"Well, it was a very interesting evening," Shelby answered.

Dawn patted the love seat cushion beside her. "We're all ears."

Despite her eagerness to get advice from her friends, April was glad for the reprieve. "What happened with Devon?"

"It was quite a scene." Shelby's expression was rueful. "He got down on his knees in the restaurant."

Jamie gasped, her hands flying up to her mouth. "To propose?"

Shelby shook her head. "I think he got carried away trying to convince me that he cared."

"But you didn't fall for it," Dawn said.

"No, I'm afraid not." Shelby's tone was decisive. "I realized that I'm completely over him." She wrinkled her nose. "He seems self-absorbed and childish to me now."

"Especially in comparison to Trevor," Jamie said shrewdly. "Where does that stand, by the way?"

"I'm not sure," Shelby said. "He wanted to have dinner tonight, but then Devon showed up. I told him that I had to talk to Devon, and Trevor seemed okay with it."

"I learned that Devon is staying at The Tidewater too," April said. "Good thing you went to Charleston for dinner."

"That's why I told Devon that I didn't want to go anywhere local," Shelby said. "But Trevor's probably written me off."

April snorted. "I doubt it. But here's a novel thought. Why not find out?"

Shelby considered for a long moment. "You're right. I have nothing to lose." She pulled out her phone and sent a text. "He probably won't get it until—"

The phone chimed.

The other women laughed.

"There's your answer," Jamie said. "He is definitely interested."

"He wants to meet for breakfast," Shelby said. "And the answer is yes." She typed her response and set the phone on the table. "Whew. That's settled."

"So, what's up with you?" Dawn asked April. She passed over a square of chocolate as if sweetening the question.

Heaving a sigh, April said, "For the most part, we had a wonderful evening. We ate dinner at Turner's Lakeside Grill. Owen is kind, intelligent, funny, and delightful to be with. The list goes on. He even took the news about my cancer in stride."

"I hear a 'but,'" Shelby said. "Was there a red flag?"

April shook her head. "Not a single one. But after he kissed me, I kind of freaked out."

"Was it awful?" Jamie asked. "Some men are terrible kissers."

"No, quite the opposite. It was a very nice first kiss." April ran a hand through her hair. "But right after, I felt terrible. My good mood collapsed like a ton of bricks."

"Hmm. Interesting." Dawn chewed a cookie. "Cold feet, maybe? Things moving a little too fast?"

April considered her friend's theory. "Well, I wanted him to kiss me, so we weren't moving too fast in that sense. I wonder if it's old rejection and fear from my broken engagement."

"I'll bet it is," Jamie said. "We have emotional memories, much like our muscle memory. You're starting to care, and last time that meant heartbreak."

"I'm such a mess," April muttered.

"No, you're not," Dawn said. "You've had a tough year."

Jamie and Shelby chimed in with reassurances.

"Owen asked me to go fishing with him tomorrow," April said. "So what should I do?"

"Do you want to see him?" Shelby asked. "If not, you don't have to. And if you do, you could tell him that you need to slow down."

"I have a feeling that he'll wait," Jamie said. "I'm sure he doesn't want to make you feel pressured."

"No, he's not like Devon," Shelby said. "Owen is a true gentleman."

While the others chatted, April ate a cookie and considered her situation. She decided that she did want to spend more time with Owen. Tonight was the most fun she'd had in years. And the idea of never seeing him again made her heart sink.

It was time to stop letting her past dictate her future.

"Okay," April blurted out, breaking into the conversation and earning startled looks. "I'm going to do it."

"Do what?" Dawn asked.

"Go fishing with Owen." Elation warred with trepidation as April picked up her phone and sent a text.

For better or worse, she was going to see Owen once more.

Shelby

Shelby entered the Dragonfly Coffee Shop and smiled when she spotted Angel behind the counter. She had been hoping that the artist would be working this morning. "It's great to see you. Wasn't the retreat amazing?"

"It sure was," Angel said. "I am so busy working on my goals. And I enjoyed making new friends. Jamie and I are going to stay in touch, help keep each other on track with our art projects."

"Fantastic." Shelby scanned the busy coffee shop. Trevor was seated in the corner, reading a book. "I'm sorry to cut our conversation short, but I'd better go. My breakfast date is waiting."

Angel followed her gaze to Trevor. "Oh, good for you." She patted Shelby's shoulder. "Weren't you with him at trivia night?"

"I was. That was our first date," Shelby said. "I hope to see you later."

"Same here," Angel said. "Enjoy your breakfast."

"Thanks." Shelby picked her way through the tables, keeping her gaze on Trevor.

When he saw her, he set his book aside with a grin.

She waved, an echoing smile breaking across her face. Was it her imagination, or had the day suddenly gotten brighter?

Trevor jumped out of his seat and pulled out a chair for her. "Glad you could make it. Have a seat, and I'll get your order. Whatever you want."

"That's so sweet. Thank you." Shelby sat down. "I'll take a large coffee with cream and a pumpkin muffin." Pumpkin was one of her favorite flavors.

"Coming right up," he said.

Shelby watched as Trevor strode toward the counter with his easy, long-limbed gait, noting how he stood back politely when an older woman got there first. While he waited to order, he began chatting with two guys at a nearby table.

Although she had enacted a mental moratorium on the subject of Devon, she couldn't help but compare the two men. She definitely preferred Trevor. Her stomach flipped over when she thought about the conversation ahead. She crossed her fingers under the table, hoping he hadn't been turned off by Devon's sudden appearance last night.

Trevor was now at the register.

Shelby occupied the time by glancing around the coffee shop and out the window at passersby on the street. Then she studied the paintings on the wall and noticed that several had been done by Angel. She was really talented. Shelby loved her use of color.

"Here we go." Trevor slid a tray onto the table, then unloaded two cups of coffee and two plates holding muffins. Napkins, cups of cream, and spoons were next. He put the empty tray on a nearby rack and sat down.

"Thank you," Shelby said. She picked up the muffin and took a big bite, tasting cinnamon and ginger and a hint of nutmeg.

Trevor added cream to his coffee, then took a sip. "I'm not even human until after my second cup of coffee."

"I hope that's not your first one," Shelby said with a laugh.

"Nope. Had one at the inn before I came over." He winked. "Count your lucky stars."

Between sips of coffee, Shelby nibbled on her muffin. "April, Jamie, Dawn, and I are staying in town until tomorrow." He'd met the other women at The Tidewater.

"I know. Dad and April are taking the boat out today." Trevor lifted a brow. "I might be mad about being displaced except for two things."

"Which are?" she prompted.

"One, I'm glad to see Dad taking an interest in someone. April's a really nice lady. And two, it gives me a chance to spend time with you."

Shelby tore her gaze from his. "I'm glad you feel that way. I'm really sorry about last night." She grimaced. "I wasn't planning on Devon showing up."

"About that," he said. "Where do you two stand?"

Now she met his eyes. "Nowhere. We're not together and never will be. We dated for a few months, but it's over."

Trevor regarded her over the rim of his cup. "So he didn't give you any trouble?"

"No, not really," Shelby said. "He wasn't happy, but he didn't have a leg to stand on and he knew it." She hesitated. How much should she share? "He cheated on me with a racetrack model."

"What?" Trevor's exclamation drew attention from around the room. With a wince, he said, "Sorry. I didn't mean to shout. But what a jerk. I can't believe anyone would cheat on you."

Shelby's heart warmed at his declaration. Every minute spent in his presence only made her like and admire him more. "Well, he did. Devon gets a lot of attention from women. It goes with the territory, I guess."

Trevor frowned but didn't make any further remarks about Devon. "So, are you okay?" He sounded tentative.

Shelby didn't blame him. Like many men, he probably wasn't eager to have a woman crying on his shoulder over someone else. "I'm fine. I really am." She drank the rest of her coffee. "Can we get a refill? That was my first cup of the day."

Trevor stood. "You bet. Today it's my job to keep you happy." He started across the floor, then halted and pivoted to face her. "By the way, I have a referral for you. For your organizing business."

As he continued on to the counter, Shelby hugged herself in elation. Not only had he remembered that she was starting a business—unlike Devon—he wanted to help her succeed. Trevor Philbrick was certainly a special man, and she felt fortunate to make his acquaintance.

He was the perfect down-to-earth antidote to her brush with fame.

April

Before April left her room to meet Owen, she remembered Winnie's gift. The two packets of toe warmers were on top of the bureau where she had left them.

How had Winnie known she would need them? Marveling at this mystery, she read the directions, opened the packets, shook them, and put them inside her boots. Within seconds, she felt welcome warmth seeping into her toes.

She pulled on a hat and gloves and grabbed her tote bag, which held an extra sweater, her water bottle, snack bars, and sunscreen. Her phone, which she could use to take pictures, went into a jacket pocket with a pair of sunglasses. She zipped them safely inside.

After one last glance around the room and one more peek into the mirror, April was ready for a day on the water. Was the woman with pink cheeks and glowing eyes really her? Was Owen responsible? Or was it the inn? There was definitely something special about this place.

April descended the stairs. When she walked out the inn's back door, she spotted the fishing boat waiting at the dock. The gleaming white craft wasn't huge, but it had elegant, powerful lines. She ambled across the grass toward it.

Owen waved from behind the console, and she waved back.

By the time she reached the waterfront, he was standing on the dock.

"Beautiful day, isn't it?" Owen said. His grin was bright in the shadow of his fishing hat.

"It sure is." Squinting against the sunlight glittering on the lake, April unzipped her pocket and removed her sunglasses. Although the air was chilly, the wind was light, barely rippling the water.

"Ready?" he asked.

She put on her sunglasses and nodded.

Owen helped her board the boat, then ushered her to the passenger seat next to the captain's chair. The boat also had two high seats, one in back and the other in front. To fish from, she guessed.

"What a beautiful boat," she said, meaning it.

That earned another big smile. "Thanks. She's my baby. Secondhand but mint."

April was pleased. His comment told her that he had good taste, was frugal, and took care of his possessions. All qualities she admired.

He poured her a cup of coffee from a thermos, made sure her water bottle was close to hand, and then took the helm, expertly backing the boat away from the dock.

Soon they turned and headed into deeper water, where Owen throttled up the engine. The outboard motor wasn't horribly loud, but it was noisy enough to discourage conversation, so April settled in the comfortable seat and sipped her coffee. Out in the middle of the lake, with sky and water all around, she started to understand why Owen loved fishing so much. It was spectacular out here.

When they reached the other side, Owen steered the boat into a large but sheltered cove. "We had good luck in here the other day. Caught some real nice bass."

"I was surprised to learn that people fish in the winter." Even in the cove, a sneaky breeze crept around April's neck. She pulled her wool hat lower on her head.

"The bass move slower, true, but so do we," Owen reasoned. "I've caught big ones in the winter. And it's nice being out here without a lot of competition." He opened a tackle box and began preparing the fishing gear.

April watched closely, asking questions.

The lure he chose was long and silver, hooked at the end. He shook it for her. "It resembles baitfish." He explained how the lure tricked fish into swallowing it.

After a few moments, she noticed he was getting two rods ready. "Am I fishing too?" She had never gone fishing in her life. A childhood aversion to the worms her friends used had helped cement that decision.

"Why not?" Owen asked. "If you want to, that is. No pressure."

April took a deep breath. She'd probably make a fool out of herself, but at least no worms were involved. "Okay, I'll try it. But I have to warn you. I'm not very coordinated."

"You don't have to be." He picked up one of the poles and guided her to the tall seat in the stern. "Are you ready for your lesson, Miss Frederick?"

April hopped up into the chair. "Certainly, Mr. Philbrick," she answered in a prim and proper voice. She sent him a mischievous look, which he returned.

As their eyes locked, April felt everything fade away. There was only Owen, his handsome face mere inches away. So easy to lean forward for another kiss . . .

Then a warning blared in her brain. Yes, something was definitely happening between them. But she wanted—no, needed—to take it very, very slowly.

"I have to tell you something," she blurted out.

Owen pulled back, the movement breaking the spell. A furrow creased his brow. "Is everything all right? You didn't get bad news, I hope."

April laughed. How wonderful that his first thought was for her health. "I'm sorry," she said, seeing confusion cloud his eyes. "I'm fine, physically. And I really, really like you. But I think we should move slowly." She put up a hand. "It's me, not you. I was burned pretty badly when I was younger, practically left at the altar. Last night after we kissed, which was lovely—well, I panicked a little."

She watched him closely, wondering how he would respond. Maybe he'd think she was too damaged, too insecure to deal with.

But after a long moment, during which he appeared to be absorbing her words, Owen said, "I'm on board with that. This is uncharted territory for me too. I was with Ellen my whole adult life. I don't want to make any mistakes or break any hearts."

Once again, their eyes locked. But this time, he smiled and said, "Ready for your lesson? The fish are waiting."

April shifted in the seat, getting more comfortable. "I sure am. Think I'll have beginner's luck?"

Grace

"I'll get that," Grace said when someone knocked on the back door. She and Charlotte were in the kitchen preparing for the dinner they were hosting. They were delighted that all the women had decided to extend their stay another night.

"Thanks," Charlotte said as she checked a vat of beans baking in the oven. She was making baked beans using their grandmother's recipe that had been found on a molasses jar.

Grace, who had been chopping vegetables for the salad, wiped her hands on her apron. "Want to come with me?" she asked Winston.

His answer was a dancing leap.

April was at the door with Owen Philbrick. They were grinning from ear to ear, and their noses were sunburned.

Winston made a beeline for April.

As April rubbed the dog's ears, she said, "We have something to add to the dinner menu."

"In there?" Grace pointed at the cooler on the doorstep. Dawn and Jamie had mentioned that April went fishing. "Did you catch something?"

"I'll say," Owen answered, hefting the cooler.

"Let's take a peek," Grace said, leading the way to the kitchen.

At Grace's direction, Owen set the cooler on a side counter, then opened the lid. "April caught this beauty."

Charlotte and Grace crowded close for the reveal. A gorgeous fish lay on top of the ice, already cleaned but head and tail intact.

"Oh my," Grace said. "It's huge."

Charlotte appeared thoughtful, probably deciding how to cook it.

"About ten pounds," Owen said. He gripped April's shoulder. "Beginner's luck for sure." The grin he exchanged with April told Grace that this was an inside joke.

"Well, it was my first time fishing," April said. "Now I'm hooked—no pun intended."

Everyone laughed.

"Told you it would happen," Owen said. "There's nothing quite like it."

"I hope you can join us for dinner tonight, Owen," Grace said. "Your son is coming."

Owen glanced at April, who nodded, smiling. "I'd love to. I'll head back to The Tidewater and get cleaned up. What time do you want us?"

"Around six would be good," Charlotte said. "We're having a social hour first and then dinner at seven."

April sniffed the air. "And it's going to be delicious. I can already tell." She patted her midsection. "I hope I can hold out until dinner."

"I'll put together a snack," Charlotte offered. "How about cheese and crackers?"

"Spending time on the water always gives you an appetite," Owen said. "I'll see you all later, and thank you for the invitation."

"I'll show you out," April said. With Winston at her heels, she walked Owen to the back door.

"So how many do we have?" Grace asked. The number kept going up, which was not a problem. The more the merrier, and Charlotte always made extra. "Winnie and Gus, Spencer, Dean, Shelby and Trevor, Jamie and Dawn, April and Owen, Maya. And us. Thirteen."

"With the fish on the menu, we'll have plenty." Charlotte stood by Owen's cooler. "Help me with this?"

Between the two of them, they carried the cooler to the counter beside the sink. There, Charlotte picked up the huge bass and set it on a board while Grace dumped the ice out of the cooler and rinsed it.

"What are you going to do with it?" Grace asked, in awe at the fish's size.

"I'm not sure yet," Charlotte said. "But whatever it is, it will be good. You can't go wrong with a beauty like this."

And you can't go wrong with a nice group like this, Grace thought.

Several hours later, the innkeepers and their guests were seated around the long table in the dining room. Flickering candles lined the middle, casting a warm glow on happy faces. The clear weather had given way to a storm, and although the wind and rain raged outside, all was snug and cozy inside the inn.

Seated at the head of the table, Grace watched as people chatted, drank wine, and enjoyed the sumptuous feast. In addition to baked bass with a light stuffing, there were steak tips, baked beans, twice-baked potatoes, and salad. Dean had brought a corn casserole, Winnie had made a pan of soft homemade rolls, and Spencer had contributed roasted pecans from his orchard for the salad. The guests had purchased flowers for the table, delivered along with a thank-you note signed by all.

April, seated at Grace's left, leaned close. "The fish is tasty, isn't it?"

"It certainly is," Grace said.

"Owen and I are going to keep seeing each other," April whispered with a smile. "But we're taking it slow. Living more than a hundred miles apart helps." She glanced with fondness at Owen, who was talking to Dean.

"Please stay in touch," Grace said. She had a good feeling about the pair. And about Shelby and Trevor, who never seemed to run out of things to talk about. The only one who seemed slightly pensive tonight was Maya, but she was doing much better than a few days ago. She seemed at peace concerning the future of her own love life.

"We sure will," April said. "My friends and I are talking about staying again next January." Her eyes sparkled with joy. "And maybe someday, Owen and I will visit together."

"I hope so," Grace said.

Shelby tapped on a glass with her knife, drawing everyone's attention. She rose, displaying a new confidence. "I have an important announcement. Trevor gave me my first organizing referral. And you're also looking at the new bookkeeper for Philbrick & Sons."

Everyone applauded.

Shelby bowed. "Thank you, Maya, the ladies of the inn, and my new friends." She grinned as she retook her seat.

"That's wonderful," Charlotte said. "We hoped this retreat would have some real results."

"It definitely did." Jamie waved an imaginary paintbrush. "I've done some of my best work ever while staying here."

"I'm writing every single day," Dawn put in. "That's a huge step for me."

April raised her hand. "Winnie, you'll be glad to know that I used those toe warmers. They were just the thing for a cold day on the lake."

Winnie's eyes twinkled. "I thought they'd come in handy."

The bell above the front door jingled.

"I'll get that." Grace put her napkin down and stood. They weren't expecting anyone tonight, and she sincerely hoped the next guests weren't early. The rooms were full until tomorrow.

A handsome older man stood in the foyer, a paper-wrapped bouquet in his hand. His hat and shoulders were wet from the driving rain. "Good evening," he said, his voice cultured and deep. Despite his well-groomed appearance, he appeared uneasy, as if unsure of his reception.

"I'm Grace Porter, one of the owners," she said. "How can I help you?"

His anxiety seemed to deepen. "Is Maya Channing still staying here?"

"She is. You must be Max."

"I am." He swallowed. "I hope she'll see me."

"I'll tell her you're here. Please follow me." Grace ushered him into the music room so the couple would have privacy for their reunion. After retrieving a towel from the half bath so he could dry off, she promised to be right back.

She quickly crossed the foyer to the dining room. Oh, how she hoped the couple would reconcile. She did love a happy ending.

Charlotte gave her a questioning look when she entered the dining room.

But Grace went straight to Maya. Bending, she whispered in her ear, "Max is here to see you. He's in the music room. What should I tell him?"

Maya pushed back the chair and got up. "Please excuse me." She practically ran from the room.

As Grace returned to her seat, Spencer asked, "Good news?"

"I believe so," Grace said, smiling. A flood of joy and gladness rushed into her heart. She picked up her glass. "Everyone, I'd like to make a toast."

"A toast," they echoed, picking up their glasses.

"To friends, family, good food, and a warm house on a stormy night," Grace said, lifting her glass.

As everyone repeated the toast, Grace whispered an addendum, "You've done it again, Magnolia Harbor Inn. Thank you."